Nothing Without You

Also from Monica Murphy

Forever Yours Series
You Promised Me Forever
Thinking About You

Damaged Hearts Series
Her Defiant Heart
His Wasted Heart
Damaged Hearts

Friends Series
One Night
Just Friends
More Than Friends
Forever: A Friends Novel

The Rules Series
Fair Game
In The Dark
Slow Play
Safe Bet

Reverie Series
His Reverie
Her Destiny

One Week Girlfriend Series
One Week Girlfriend
Second Chance Boyfriend
Three Broken Promises
Drew + Fable Forever
Four Years Later
Five Days Until You

Billionaire Bachelors Club Series
Crave
Torn
Savor

Intoxicated

The Fowler Sisters Series
Owning Violet
Stealing Rose
Taming Lily

The Never Series
Never Tear Us Apart
Never Let You Go

Young Adult Standalones
Daring The Bad Boy
Saving It
Pretty Dead Girls

Nothing Without You
By Monica Murphy

A Forever Yours/Big Sky Novella

Introduction by Kristen Proby

EVIL EYE
CONCEPTS

Nothing Without You: A Forever Yours/Big Sky Novella
By Monica Murphy
Copyright 2019
ISBN: 978-1-970077-12-4

Published by Evil Eye Concepts, Incorporated

An Introduction to the Kristen Proby Crossover Collection

Everyone knows there's nothing I love more than a happy ending. It's what I do for a living–I'm in LOVE with love. And what's better than love? More love, of course!

Just imagine, Louis Vuitton and Tiffany, collaborating on the world's most perfect handbag. Jimmy Choo and Louboutin, making shoes just for me. Not loving it enough? What if Hugh Grant in *Notting Hill* was the man to barge into Sandra Bullock's office in *The Proposal?* I think we can all agree that Julia Roberts' character would have had her hands full with Ryan Reynolds.

Now imagine what would happen if one of the characters from my Big Sky Series met up with other characters from some of your favorite authors' series. Well, wonder no more because The Kristen Proby Crossover Collection is here, and I could not be more excited!

Rachel Van Dyken, Laura Kaye, Sawyer Bennett, Monica Murphy, Samantha Young, and K.L. Grayson are all bringing their own beloved characters to play – and find their happy endings – in my world. Can you imagine all the love, laughter and shenanigans in store?

I hope you enjoy the journey between worlds!

Love,
Kristen Proby

The Kristen Proby Crossover Collection features a new novel by Kristen Proby and six by some of her favorite writers:

Kristen Proby – Soaring with Fallon
Sawyer Bennett – Wicked Force
KL Grayson – Crazy Imperfect Love
Laura Kaye – Worth Fighting For
Monica Murphy – Nothing Without You
Rachel Van Dyken – All Stars Fall
Samantha Young – Hold On

Acknowledgments from the Author

This collection wouldn't have happened without (of course!) Kristen Proby, so thank you so much Kristen, for asking me to do this. You're a great friend and a smart businesswoman—writing my story in your world was so much fun, and I'm so honored to be included in this collection with you and all of the authors involved. A huge thank you as well to Liz Berry—you are so sweet and your enthusiasm is catching! I'm excited to be a part of the 1001 Dark Nights family.

Sign up for the 1001 Dark Nights Newsletter
and be entered to win a Tiffany Lock necklace.

There's a contest every quarter!

Go to www.1001DarkNights.com to subscribe.

As a bonus, all subscribers can download
FIVE FREE exclusive books!

Chapter One

Maisey

"Tucker McCloud is back in town."

I nearly drop the cake pan I'm carrying over to the counter at my older sister's nonchalant statement. I set it down with a loud plop, glaring at Brooke.

She doesn't even bother lifting her head. She's too busy studying her phone screen, scrolling through Facebook.

It's a Sunday afternoon and for some reason, I was full of nervous energy, so I decided to mess around in the kitchen like I do and come up with new cake flavors. When I texted Brooke to come over, she didn't even hesitate.

"Are you serious right now?" I practically screech, then take a deep breath.

No biggie. No big deal. Nope, I don't care that Tucker's back in town. It's probably a rumor. It's happened before. The residents of Cunningham Falls are always eager to welcome back their hometown boy who made good. The first football player from our high school to ever sign with the NFL, he's a big deal around here.

Not to me, though. I'd rather pretend he never even existed.

"His sister posted a photo of him last night," Brooke says, her eyes still glued to her phone screen.

I walk over to where she's standing, ignoring my rapidly beating heart. When she still doesn't bother looking up, I thrust my hand between her face and her phone, snapping my fingers. She hates it when I do that. "Brooke."

Brooke's head snaps up, her brown eyes narrow. "What?"

"Show me the photo." My voice is surprisingly calm, considering how jittery I suddenly feel.

She goes to the search box, enters in Tucker's sister's name—Stella McCloud—and clicks on Stella's profile. "Looks like they had a family get-together over the weekend, and Tucker came home for it," she explains as she starts scrolling, looking for those photos. "Ah, here they are—"

I snatch the phone out of her hand before she can say anything else, earning an irritated "Hey!" for my efforts, but I ignore her. I'm too hell bent on finding the photo of Tucker.

Brooke's right, I realize as I start examining each and every photo—forty-eight in all. There was definitely a family get-together over the weekend for the McCloud clan, and let me tell you, their clan is a big one. They're one of the largest families in the area. Tucker has lots of siblings—six besides him—and he's smack dab in the middle. The middle child always craves attention. It's a known fact.

And Tucker was the biggest attention hog I knew. From his antics on the football field and on social media, I'm guessing that's still true.

I stop on a photo of the entire family gathered together, and I spot him immediately. Very back row, on the far right. Tall and imposing with those broad shoulders and the light brown hair and the laughing eyes. Ugh.

He's still ridiculously good looking.

It's *so* annoying.

The photos are endless, and I'm surprised to see every single McCloud sibling is there. Only three out of the six remain in town, including Stella, the youngest. She's a teacher at the local elementary school, and Wyatt is the football coach at the high school in the next town over. Wyatt is considered one of the most appealing bachelors left in the area—thirty-four, still single, attractive and with a good job. Women call him the uncatchable catch.

Just like his stupid twin brother, Tucker.

My ex-boyfriend. My high school sweetheart. The boy who took me to all the big dances, who made out with me in the cab of his truck after every single game, who snuck through my window in the middle of the night so he could sleep with me, even for just an hour. The first boy to tell me he loved me. The boy who gave me my first orgasm. The boy who told me he couldn't breathe if he didn't have me in his life.

This is the same boy who got a football scholarship from a D-1 school and broke up with me, all in the same day. So excuse the above facts I just listed. He didn't take me to *all* the big dances. I didn't go to his senior prom, but neither did he.

Little consolation for how badly he destroyed me.

"He looks great, right?" Brooke says, her innocent question breaking through my nostalgic thoughts. "Actually, they all do. The McClouds are a good-looking bunch."

I pause on a photo of the brothers, four in all. Hunter, Colton, Tucker, and Wyatt, their arms around each other's shoulders, matching smiles on their faces. Yes, they're all attractive. Hunter and Colton are both married, and Hunter already has children. The twins are single and handsome, but only one McCloud makes my heart thump wildly and my breath catch.

And all I'm doing is looking at a photo of him on Facebook, for the love of God.

"He looks phony," I say as I hand the phone back to Brooke, the only insult I can come up with in my muddled-by-Tucker brain. It's starting to hit me that we're in the same state. We're in the same town. I could bump into him at any given moment and I wonder what I might do if that happened. Hug him?

Or punch him in the face?

"Phony?" Brooke actually snorts, something she normally doesn't do. My older sister has her shit together. She owns Brooke's Blooms, and she is the most popular florist in town. Oh, and she just so happens to be married to one of the hottest men alive, Brody Chabot. They are so in love, it's a little sickening.

Fine, I'm just jealous.

"Slick. Almost too perfect," I say, redefining my phony statement. "Look at his hair." He has amazing hair. Soft. He liked it when I ran my fingers through it. I'd be sitting on the couch and he'd rest his head in my lap, staring up at me with his beautiful blue eyes, practically begging me to stroke his hair. And I always would…

Brooke comes to stand beside me, peering over my shoulder. "At least he still has hair."

"Why wouldn't he?" I ask incredulously, wondering if I'd still find Tucker attractive even if he was bald. Probably. "He's not that old."

"There were a lot of guys at my ten-year reunion who were already balding," Brooke points out. "You said the same thing about yours."

Tucker didn't even show up to Brooke's ten-year reunion—they graduated in the same class. "What does that have to do with anything?"

"I don't know." She shrugs. "I'm trying not to focus on his extraordinarily good-looking face."

Huh. Of course, this means I have to stare at his extraordinarily good-looking face. And my sister's right. He's so freaking hot.

I hate him.

"And his body. I mean, did you see the endorsement he had with that one underwear line a couple years ago? We pretty much saw everything." I glance up at her just in time to see her wrinkle her nose. "Some things I didn't want to see, too."

"Like what?" I saw the photos from the underwear campaign. I might have a secret board on Pinterest where I can study them on rare occasions.

"Like the outline of his—" Brooke points down below. "Junk. Some things I don't want to know, Maise."

Now it's my turn to grimace. "Some things I don't really want to know either, Brooke. Like you have an idea of what Tucker's junk looks like."

"I definitely know his junk is nothing to sneeze at." Brooke bursts out laughing the second she says the words. "I can't believe we're having this conversation."

"You're the one who brought it up!" I'm tempted to go on my phone and look at those photos again. I'm friends with Stella too. We were close in school. We still occasionally get together for lunch or drinks, and we talk about everything and everyone with the exception of Tucker.

Stella knows he's off limits.

"You think he already went back to California?" I ask when Brooke hasn't said anything.

"Why? Hoping you'll run into him?" Brooke smiles, her eyes sparkling. She just got back from her honeymoon and she's so happy. Wedded bliss looks good on her. Looks good on her husband, too. Brody can't stop smiling either. It's so sweet to see them together.

Makes me a little bit envious. I wish I could find someone like Brody. It's hard, though, when I'm so busy making wedding cakes for all the other blissed-out couples in town getting married.

Speaking of wedding cakes…

"I need to frost this thing," I say, grabbing the cake pan and setting it on the cooling rack. "And then I want you to give it a try."

"You should've invited Brody over to sample it."

"Um…" I hesitate, not wanting to offend. "He kind of makes me nervous," I say with a wince.

Brooke glances up, her expression surprised. "But why? He loves everything you make."

"I don't know." I shrug. "I want him to be honest with me."

"He's always honest."

"He likes everything I bake. Even the gross stuff."

Brooke laughs. "He's easy to please when it comes to sweets."

"Uh huh." My voice is dripping with sarcasm and I grab the bowl full of frosting I made earlier. It's just the base. I'm going to add a few things to it now to correspond with the cake. "You're honest. You tell me if what you just ate is total crap."

"Nothing you make is ever crap, and you know it," Brooke says with all that older sister authority she's so good at delivering. "Sometimes, you get a little—out there with your flavors, but that's always in good fun. You know what works for your business and you stick with it."

"You might not say that about the cake I'm going to serve you here in a bit." It's orange. As in, it's flavored with orange, the cake itself is bright orange, and the frosting is going to have a hint of orange flavor, as well as a pale orange color. Simple, right? But kind of daring, because orange cake is hardly ever ordered anymore. It's always lemon. Sometimes strawberry, though that can be terribly sweet.

Orange is from the seventies. Mom still fantasizes about some orange Bundt cake she ate when she was a kid at someone's birthday party. She wants to find the duplicate of that cake. So when I'm bored, I go in search of it, trying to recreate her memories of sunshine and summer—that's how she describes the taste of the cake. Later tonight, I'll bring Mom a slice.

If it's any good, that is.

"I'm not worried," Brooke says with all the assuredness in the world. I appreciate her total belief in me. I always have. We've always been super close. Only a year apart in school, we shared friends, though never boyfriends, thank goodness. That would just be too weird.

Tucker was in her class, and so was Brody. Brody and Tucker were friends, though they didn't necessarily hang out together. Brody pretty much kept to himself. Brooke explained everything to me right before they got married, confessing that his father was a total monster. So he distanced himself from everyone, including Brooke.

Yet look at them now.

Sighing happily, I reach for the tiny bottle of orange extract and twist off the cap, adding a couple of drops to the vanilla frosting. I have a small bowl full of orange zest I made earlier, and I grab a pinch, sprinkling it into the bowl. Then I grab a spoon and start stirring.

"Not using your mixer?" Brooke asks.

"This one is—delicate," I tell her, hoping she understands. "I have to get the flavors balanced just right. I'd rather do it by hand."

"The master at work." Brooke rises to her feet and starts to exit my kitchen, coming to a stop right beside me so she can press a quick kiss to my cheek. "I want a slice, but I have to go."

I pause in my stirring. "You didn't even get to taste it yet."

"Brody just texted me, asking if I'd meet him for dinner, so I need to go home and take a shower. He mentioned he has a surprise for me." She smiles. "You should join us."

Frowning, I shake my head. "What if your surprise is his—penis wrapped in neon pink paper?"

Brooke laughs, covering her mouth with her hand. "Seriously, Maisey! We're meeting for *dinner*. In public. He's not going to present me his penis at the dinner table."

This conversation just took a weird and confusing turn. "You never know," I mumble, my cheeks hot. I don't want to go to dinner with them. Oh, I know they'll include me in their conversations and make it be about the three of us versus the two of them, but still. I'll feel like a third wheel. Witnessing their love is beautiful yet pathetic.

As in, they make a beautiful couple. And they make me feel pathetic.

"You're being ridiculous." Another kiss on the cheek from my sister and then she's gone, the scent of her flowery perfume still lingering in the kitchen. "I'm going to text you later!" she calls as she opens the front door. "Convince you to come to dinner with us!"

"And be the tag-along little sister during your romantic dinner where he gives you a surprise? No, thanks," I mutter under my breath, ignoring how my arm aches. My date tonight is with my kitchen and this orange cake. That way I can be alone with my thoughts.

My Tucker McCloud-filled thoughts.

Chapter Two

Tucker

I'm lurking around the oldest, smallest grocery store in Cunningham Falls on a Sunday night. The same store my mom used to always shop at when we were kids, when there weren't many options. I remember coming here a lot, all of us driving Mom crazy when we'd argue over who gets to ride in the cart, or who gets to pick this week's cereal. Doing my best to be good so I could get a treat at the end of the shopping excursion. That treat usually involved a candy bar, or ice cream in the summertime. On the rare occasion we'd get a donut, and they were always warm, just out of the oven.

That's what the store is known for. The bakery makes fresh donuts until eight o'clock every evening. The locals pile in looking for their fix on a daily basis. And seeing the line of obvious tourists at the counter at this very moment, looks like the out-of-towners know to come here too.

The smell of fresh donuts hits me now as I sail past the bakery, tugging my hat low so hopefully no one will recognize me. I don't want any trouble. I'm here in Cunningham Falls to lay low and pretend I'm not Tucker McCloud, NFL football star. I'm just Tucker, middle son of the McCloud family, fraternal twin to my brother Wyatt. No one special, nothing to see here, move along, people. My time in my hometown is indefinite. I could leave tomorrow, I could stay for six weeks. I have nothing—and no one—to return to. Not even a pet.

If anyone depended on me to live, I'd definitely kill them. No joke.

And that's okay. I like being independent. I don't need a woman, or a relationship, or a dog, or even a pet fish. I haven't had a long-term relationship in years. Not even a short-term relationship. When I first joined the NFL, I had so many gorgeous women coming at me I didn't *need* a relationship. Who wants the same old thing when you can sample a different woman every single night?

As the years went by and I got traded to different teams a few times, I realized I didn't want the pressure of a relationship. It's tough having a girlfriend when you don't know where you're going to play next season. And you travel a lot. You might own a house or a condo, but you don't really own any furniture beyond a bed and maybe a couch. I have no domestic skills—well, I did when I was a kid and had to help out around the house, but before last night, I don't remember the last time I had to wash a dish or sweep a floor.

My oldest sister Georgia is a task master. After Mom's birthday dinner, she made all of us clean our parents' kitchen, which sucked. Made me feel like a little kid again, being bossed around by my big sister—who I tower over, thank you very much. She also gave us single McClouds a lecture on finding ourselves and being mature, responsible adults. I reminded her that I paid off Mom and Dad's mortgage, so if that doesn't make me responsible, I don't know what does, but she didn't comment. Just gave me that tight-lipped, older sister judging look that made me want to do something stupid.

Like run and tell on her to Mom.

Seriously, I'm in my thirties, and I've finally settled down. Somewhat. It's been three seasons and I've remained in San Francisco—more accurately, Santa Clara—and I recently bought a house. No pets though. Still don't have a girlfriend either. I'm finally over the different-girl-every-night plan. That got old. And to be honest, I'm getting old.

As in, older and wiser.

Why am I thinking about my lack of relationships while I wander the aisles of this freezing cold grocery store? Maybe it's because my entire family has been asking way too many questions since I arrived a few days ago. They all want to know what's going on with me, how's my love life, when am I ever going to get married?

Married? Are they insane? That's the *last* thing I want to do. Let me get through a couple more seasons with the NFL and then I'll consider something long-term.

Maybe.

I'm lingering by the bakery, contemplating ordering a dozen donuts and not really paying attention when I run into someone. A soft, fragrant little someone who barks out a sharp *hey* when I knock into her. Every hair on my body seems to stand on end at hearing that voice.

That very familiar, irritated voice.

I glance down and see her. See the bent head and the long, dark hair, and the way her black T-shirt stretches across her chest and yep, I know her. I know her very, very well.

"Oh. My. God. I knew this would happen," Maisey Henderson mutters under her breath, shaking her head as she steps away from me. She keeps stepping away, as if she needs the distance, and I quickly realize my idea of a welcoming hug and pleasant reunion with my high school sweetheart is out of the question.

Someone is clearly pissed by my mere presence.

"Maisey." That's all I say. Just her name. I let her glare up at me as I take her in, and hot damn, she looks good. Even better than the last time I saw her, and that's been a while. And good is an understatement. Maisey looks...*amazing.* Short and curvy with that gorgeous thick hair and that pretty, pretty face.

"Tucker." She spits out my name like a dirty word. "I heard you were back in town."

"From who?" I ask incredulously, though I guess I shouldn't be surprised. I've been away for so long, you tend to forget just how small your small town can be.

"Stella." Maisey lifts her head, her nose in the air. I always thought she had a cute nose. She has a cute everything. "She posted photos this weekend. On Facebook."

Stella. My baby sister. The one who organized this family reunion of sorts to begin with. "We all got together for my mom. It was her birthday," I say. Why do I feel dumbstruck by her presence? My brain is going a million miles a minute with all the things I could say, all of them about her.

You're still beautiful.

You're still sassy.

Are you mad at me?

Are you single?

"Oh," Maisey returns coolly, shifting her weight from one foot to the other. She's got a small brown bottle of something clutched in her hand, and I wonder what it is. "How is your mother?"

"She's doing great." And she is. My parents have been married for almost forty years—their anniversary is coming up soon. Dad joked he married her right after her birthday so he wouldn't forget the date, and I half believe him.

"Tell her I said hi." Maisey starts to walk past me, a fake smile barely curling her lush lips. "Good seeing you, Tucker. Have a nice life."

"Hey, hey, hey." I grab her arm, halting her escape. She turns, her gaze on the spot where my fingers press into her arm—and yes, there's electricity sparking, I wonder if she feels it too—before returning her gaze to mine. "So that's it? That's all you're going to say?"

"What do you expect me to say?" She pulls away from me and I drop my hand, hating the tone of her voice, the anger I hear there. The glare in her eyes as she blinks up at me. "You want me to gush over your success? Tell you how great you look? Because you look pretty great, Tucker. Not that you don't already know this."

I can't help but puff out my chest a little bit. Maisey thinks I look great.

"There's nothing else for me to say," she continues irritably and I deflate, just like that. "We broke up, it was over, I never heard from you again. And now, all these years later, we literally bump into each other at the grocery store, and all I can say is, *have a nice life*. I think that's pretty civil of me, don't you agree?"

No way am I going to answer that question. Instead, I change the subject. "You want to get together sometime this week? Have dinner? Catch up?"

Her mouth pops open in what I guess is shock. "No. I do not."

What the hell? I'm speechless.

"Bye." She flaps her fingers at me in a hostile wave and then she's gone.

Like a jackass, I turn and watch her walk away, my gaze dropping to her swishing hips, that perfect ass that's yep, still perfect. I let her go before. Hell, back in the day I ended it first, thinking it was the best thing for us.

I can admit now that I was young and a complete idiot.

Determination filling me, I head for the bakery, ready to order a dozen—no, fuck that, I want *two* dozen donuts. I'll take the giant pink box back to Mom and Dad's, invite Stella over so I can bribe her with a maple bar, and interrogate her until I find out everything I need to know about Maisey Henderson.

And maybe somehow, some way, I can convince Maisey that I truly am sorry for what I did to her when we were kids.

Chapter Three

Maisey

"My brother wants me to convince you that he's really a good guy," Stella says as her way of greeting when I answer my phone Monday morning.

My stomach flutters at the mention of Stella's brother. This means Tucker has been talking about me. To his sister. Maybe to other members of his family as well. I shouldn't like this. I should be irritated.

But deep down, I sort of like it.

Fine. I *really* like it. His talking about me means he's also thinking about me. And I'm thinking about him. What does this mean?

Nothing really.

I guess.

"He's a jerk," I tell her as I collapse onto my couch. I usually don't go into work on Mondays unless I have an appointment with a client. I have exactly one appointment at three that came across my website appointment scheduler late last night, and it's for an anniversary cake. Which isn't that unusual, but I normally meet with engaged couples planning their wedding. This appointment should be—every pun intended—a piece of cake. "And you can tell Tucker I said that."

Stella laughs. "No way. That'll make him want me to convince you even more."

"Convince me of what? I don't know why I need convincing." It was so weird to see Tucker last night. I needed more orange extract and I went to our local grocery store that carries a variety of things you don't see at the average supermarket. I found what I was looking for, was ready to hustle my butt out of there, and instead, my butt collided with a solid wall of man muscle.

Tucker McCloud.

"He thinks you hate him," Stella tells me.

"He's right. I do hate him," I say without hesitation.

Stella heaves an irritated sigh. "You do not. You're over him, remember?"

I do remember telling Stella that back in high school. I told all of my friends that because otherwise, I looked pitiful. And I didn't want to be that girl, sad and heartbroken over her older boyfriend who dumped her and took off to college to become a huge sensation. That wasn't me.

I pretended instead. Acted like I moved on, that I was having fun. It was my senior year! Time to live it up before reality set in.

No one knew I nursed a broken heart for most of that year, with the exception of my sister. Brooke has always been there for me.

Jeez. Brooke. I need to tell her I ran into him.

"Fine, I don't hate him," I admit to Stella when I realize she's waiting for me to say something. "But I don't necessarily want to be his friend either."

"Why not?"

"Why should I? This is the first time I've seen him here in *years*." I stress the last word. "I'm assuming he never comes home to visit you guys like, ever?"

"He came home for Mom's birthday because I guilt tripped him into doing it," Stella confesses. "The guy is never around for any holiday function. Like ever."

"Right. No surprise." He's a total disappointment to the family, I'm sure.

"It's because he really is busy. He sends the most elaborate gifts for all of us for our birthdays and Christmas. He does take care of us." Stella hesitates. "But I told him he needs to actually show his face here once in a while. I made him feel guilty."

"Good." I am a rude, awful person for saying that out loud.

"He's not a bad person, Maise. Mom and Dad are so proud of him." I can hear the pride tinge her voice too. The McClouds are all proud of Tucker's success. As well they should be. The guy is an NFL sensation. A great player who is paid well, and I'm sure he'll take care of his family as best as he can as long as the money keeps rolling in.

"Of course they are."

"He paid off their mortgage. Paid off Georgia's too. Tried to pay off Hunter's, but he wouldn't let him," Stella continues.

"Oh. Wow. That's so generous." He was always giving toward me when we were together, but that was a lifetime ago. We might've been a couple for two years, but your wants and needs are so different when you're a teen versus now as we deal with adulthood. I'm glad Tucker is taking care of his family.

Yet I can't help but remember how he took care of me too…

"You won't meet with him? Go to dinner with him?" Stella asks hopefully.

I laugh. "How much is he paying you to ask me this?"

"Nothing, I swear! I just—I know he feels bad about how he ended things with you," Stella explains.

"He should feel bad. He broke my heart." That I can say it so casually makes me feel like I am totally over what he did to me. I'm not holding a grudge.

Okay, maybe I'm holding the *tiniest* grudge, but seriously. Dinner? With Tucker? Make myself crazy staring at him from across a table while he sweet talks me the entire evening?

I don't know if I'd have the willpower to resist him. He could probably snap his fingers and have me any way he wants me. Maybe.

I'm not sure.

And for that reason alone, I have to pass. To save myself.

"He was young and stupid," Stella says.

"We were all young and stupid. It's what happens when you're in high school." I sigh, my gaze going to the window. I should take a walk. Burn some calories while I stew over Tucker and his ridiculous requests. "Tell him thank you from me. I really do appreciate it. But…I'm not interested."

The moment I say those words, I have regret.

I'm not interested sounds like a lie. Maybe because…

It *is* a lie. Despite everything, I'm still interested. And curious.

So curious.

We talk a few more minutes, idle chitchat about nothing much, and then finally…

The conversation is over.

And hopefully I won't have to deal with Tucker McCloud invading my life ever again.

* * * *

I enter Cake Nation at two-fifty-two, breathless and harried, flicking on lights, running back to my tiny office to grab my appointment book and a notepad. I might be a modern businesswoman of the twenty-first century, but I still like to handwrite my client notes, and I keep track of appointments in my planner. Something about writing everything down that helps stick information in my brain, I guess.

I'm still in my office, shuffling through the stack of mail I forgot to look at over the weekend, when I hear the overhead bell ring, indicating someone has entered the building.

"Just a minute," I call before I head back out into the main reception area of Cake Nation.

The building I've leased is small, but it's all mine, and it's right next to my sister's flower shop, which is handy when we meet potential wedding clients. I have an industrial kitchen that takes up most of the space, allowing for all the baking I need to do, and the lobby/meeting area of Cake Nation is very small, yet cozy. I don't sell baked goods to the public on a daily basis. Mine is more a caterer-type bakery, and it works for me.

The ultimate dream is to have an actual bakery with a glass case displaying the various cakes, cookies, and pies I create, along with breakfast pastries. Maybe I could offer up coffee, too. Keep it open through lunchtime and have sandwiches, paninis…

Dreams. I have lots of them.

"Hey, Maise."

I come to an abrupt stop when I see who's standing in the middle of my tiny, cozy spot.

Freaking Tucker.

"What are you doing here?" I snap. His eyebrows lower in that glowering way of his, but I'm not deterred. "Please tell me Stella didn't send you."

"Stella didn't send me," he says, frowning. "And is that any way to greet a potential client?"

My mouth pops open. "Potential client?"

"I made an appointment. With that handy appointment page you have on your website."

Wait. What? "You're my three o'clock?" Oh my God. He used a

fake name. I glance at my planner, where I wrote Nancy and Bob, 3 p.m.

Nancy and Bob McCloud. Tucker's parents.

I'm going to kill him.

Tucker nods in response to my question. Rubs his hand along his jaw, and I swear I can hear the rasping of his whiskers from here. Not that there's a huge amount of distance between us. Remember what I said? About Cake Nation being small and cozy?

Yeah. Tucker is anything but small, and he feels extra close. In fact, his mere presence is eating up all the space, and his overwhelming gravitational pull is tugging me in. Pulling me closer.

I try my best to resist, but it's difficult. Without thought, I step closer, until I'm standing directly in front of him, and I can smell his delicious, intoxicating scent.

For a moment, I sort of forget about everything, and just enjoy the fact that Tucker is here. With me. In my place of business—the place of my dreams.

But then I remember that he is my next potential client and I need to remain strictly business.

"Why did you make an appointment using your parents' names?" I ask him.

"I need an anniversary cake." He shrugs. "And I knew you wouldn't meet with me if I said your appointment was with me."

He's right about that, but I'm still a little confused. I blame Tucker. For existing. "Who do you need the anniversary cake for?"

"My parents. Bob and Nancy." He smiles, and it completely transforms his face. His smile is adorable, reminding me of a time when he was young and sweet and all mine. "They're going to celebrate their fortieth not this weekend but the next one."

"Oh. Forty years? How wonderful." I blink at him, then turn and sit on the pale blue velvet sofa, grabbing my planner and flipping it open. "Unfortunately, I have two weddings that weekend."

I'm trying my best to sound extra disappointed, but truthfully, I'm relieved that I'm not available to make and deliver that cake. The more distance between Tucker and me, the better. I don't want him back in my life.

He complicates things. Just by existing.

"Are those two weddings on Saturday?" he asks just before he settles on the sofa.

Right next to me.

He's so close, I can feel his body heat radiating, drawing me in.

"Yes. Saturday." I nod, feeling like a dummy. I wish he'd chosen the chair. He's so close.

Too close.

"I know this is sort of last minute, but Georgia was talking about how great your cakes are, and Stella said we should ask if you're available. Luckily for us, their anniversary party is on Sunday. Oh, and it's a surprise, so you can't tell anyone, especially Mom and Dad." He leans forward, resting his elbows on his knees, and turns his head, contemplating me. "Whatcha think? You up for it?"

My logical brain screams, *No! Don't do it! Tell him to get the hell out of your business—and your life!*

But my heart…

And my body…

"Sure. I'll do it," I say with a tremulous smile.

Yeah. My heart and body have different ideas.

Chapter Four

Tucker

That smile Maisey is aiming at me is like an electric zing straight to my heart, amped up at full voltage. I take a deep breath and smile at her in return, ignoring my body's instant reaction to her easy, sexy smile.

Because damn, the woman is sexy. Maisey at sixteen had stolen my heart, but this version of Maisey could probably steal my damn soul if I don't watch it. She smells amazing, and her eyes are so dark—full of mystery. Secrets I want to know. She's curvy in all the right places, and she's actually a business owner, which I happen to think is…

Pretty hot.

To be honest, I didn't expect her ready agreement to make the cake for my parents' anniversary party. I'd been fully prepared to hear a resounding no. And I wouldn't blame her for refusing me, either. If she's still pissed, which I think she might be, then I can't change her feelings.

But to harbor a grudge for that long has to mean something, am I right? My mama always said there's a thin line between love and hate.

"You're serious about making their cake," I say when I realize she's waiting for me to respond.

"I am." She sighs, glances down at her planner, and starts writing something in one of the little squares. "I don't know why, but I am."

"This is great, Maise. Really. You don't know how much I appreciate it. How much my entire family appreciates it." I sit up straighter, run a hand through my hair, my brain full of sudden, over-the-top cake ideas. Like maybe I want to impress her or something? As if I have cake decorating knowledge?

Give me a break.

But I plow ahead anyway.

"For the cake, I was thinking something elaborate," I start, noting how her delicate brows draw together just before she drops her gaze to her planner once more. She used to do that when we were together too, the eyebrow thing. Some things just don't change. "A completely over-the-top themed cake to celebrate my parents. Married couples rarely make it to forty years, you know?"

"True." She pauses, turning to look at me with those huge, chocolate brown eyes. "How elaborate were you thinking?"

"Maybe you can make tiers? Five of them?"

Uh oh. She's frowning. "*Five?*"

"Maybe four," I say in a rush, changing my tune. Maybe I'm asking for too much. "Four tiers to represent forty years. That's a good idea, don't you think?"

Right? God, I know nothing about cakes. She's the expert. I should let her do all the talking and planning. Or get my sisters in on it.

They wanted in on it. Stella wanted to meet with Maisey without me and I refused. Half the point of me coming to this appointment was to talk to Maise. Like I'd hand it over to Stella to take care of?

Get real.

"I was thinking more along the lines of a sheet cake. Maybe two? One to represent your mom and one for your dad? I guess it all depends on how many people you're inviting to the party," she suggests.

"A sheet cake?" *Boring.* "And this party is going to be huge. We only came up with the party idea a few days ago, and we're pretty much inviting the entire town."

"Of course you are," she says dryly, setting her planner on the coffee table in front of us. "Give me a minute and let me go grab my portfolio. Hopefully you can get some inspiration from my previous work."

I watch her rise to her feet, openly ogling her as she walks away. She's wearing a dress. Tiny white flowers on a red background, the skirt stopping just above her knees. The fabric hugs her curves in all the right places, emphasizing the perfection that is her ass, and my gaze lingers there. Remembers touching it. Walking the hallways at school with my hand firmly planted on it, as if I were staking my claim.

And I was. Always so damn proud to call Maisey Henderson mine...

Until I dumped her like a complete dumbass.

What would've happened if we'd stayed together? Would we have lasted? Maybe she would've followed me and we'd have gone to college together. Lived together. I might've asked her to marry me right before the NFL draft. Changing teams and cities would've been hard on her, but we could've made it work, as long as we had each other. Hell, if we'd stuck together, we could have a couple of kids by now. A girl who looks just like her and a wild little boy just like me—

"Here you go."

I blink to find Maisey standing there, trying to hand me a white binder. I take it from her with clumsy hands—and I never have clumsy hands, it's my job to catch fucking footballs for the love of God. I flick open the portfolio, my eyes widening when I see the photos laid out before me.

Simple white frosted wedding cakes with fresh flowers winding a path down the tiers. A pale purple tiered cake dotted with delicate butterflies suspended by thin wire, appearing ready to take flight. Another white cake, two square tiers trimmed in gold leaf.

I turn the pages slowly, remaining quiet as I take her work in. These aren't just cakes, they're like little works of art. Too beautiful to eat.

Though I bet they taste damn good.

"Your cakes..." My voice drifts as I keep flipping the pages, taking in the artistry, the variety, the smiling faces of the occasional bride and groom posing next to their cakes. Cakes Maisey created for their special days.

"My cakes what?" she asks, and I hear the nervousness in her voice, catch the way she's clutching her hands together in her lap when I glance up to find her sitting next to me on the couch once more.

I didn't even realize she'd sat down. I was too entranced with her photos.

"They're amazing," I tell her, lifting my head so my gaze meets hers. I want her to know I mean what I say. "They're like art."

Her cheeks flush and the pleased closed-mouth smile curling her lips makes me happy. "Thank you."

"I mean it. They're beautiful. And I never think cake is beautiful." I sort through the pages, searching for one cake in particular, slapping the page with my palm when I find it. "I think I want a cake like this for my parents."

She scoots closer to me, her hair brushing against my shoulder when she peers down at the page I'm indicating. The cake is constructed of three square tiers, frosted in white and gold and black. It's something Mom would like, I just know it.

"Art Deco style?" Maisey leans in, tapping the photo with her index finger. Her nail is short, and painted a pale pink. "Like The Great Gatsby? I loved that movie."

"My mom did too. She's redone their bedroom over the years to have that mirrored look. Straight lines everywhere. Lots of gold." An idea forms in my head. "Maybe we should make it a costume party."

"But I thought it was a surprise party?" She sits up straight, turning her head so her gaze meets mine once again, and our faces are so close.

Almost kissing close.

"I'm sure we can put something together without them knowing exactly what's going on." Maybe we can. Or maybe I can just sit here and stare at Maisey's lips for the rest of the afternoon. They're full and pink, formed in the slightest pout, and I remember her taste. How sweet her kisses were. How much I enjoyed kissing her.

We did a lot of things when we were teenagers, but we never actually did the deed. I've kissed that mouth for hours, though. I bet all those hours add up to days. Weeks. Maybe even months.

"Where's the party at?" she asks, sounding the tiniest bit breathless.

Like maybe my nearness is having as much of an effect on her as having her so close is on me.

I mention the very hotel I'm staying at near the lake—it has a giant ballroom—and Maisey nods her approval, scooting away from me. Guess we're back to business. "That'll be perfect. Let me work on a sketch tonight and I'll send it to you. Maybe via email?"

"You can text it to me, if that works," I suggest, wanting to get her number.

She's a little hesitant at first, but eventually she's got my phone in her hands, adding her name and number to my contacts. I take the phone from her when she's done, sending her the quickest text, and then she's hustling me out of her little cake shop, the door closing with a firm slam behind me.

I'm left standing on the sidewalk, blinking against the intense late afternoon sun, my head spinning, my body vibrating with need.

Yeah. I'm not ready to go back to California yet. I have some unfinished business to attend to here in Cunningham Falls.

And that unfinished business has everything to do with Maisey.

Chapter Five

Maisey

"So." Brooke leans against my kitchen counter, a wineglass dangling from her fingers. Her smile is smug, the smile of a woman who is happy, confident, and madly in love. "You haven't filled me in on the details about your encounter with Tucker yesterday."

Ugh. I want to punch her in her too-happy face.

Wait. That's not true. I don't want to hurt my sister. Finally she's in a place in life where everything is going her way, and no one deserves it more than her. I would never admit this out loud, but I'm a little envious. Yeah, yeah, my life is good. I'm pleased with how quickly my business is growing. I have a cute duplex I rent and I'm saving money in the hopes to eventually expand my business and maybe, possibly buy a house someday soon. A little fixer-upper. Something cute and charming and all mine.

But right now, those things are just...dreams. Future visions on my imaginary vision board.

Hmmm. Maybe I *should* make a vision board. If you put it out there, eventually all of your dreams will come true—

"Maise." Brooke snaps her fingers right in front of my face, startling me.

"What?" I blink at her, then blindly reach for my own wineglass to find that it's empty.

I immediately grab the wine bottle sitting nearby and pour myself another glass.

"Your meeting. With Tucker. How did it go? What did he say? What did *you* say?" Clearly Brooke is repeating herself, and getting annoyed with me too.

"How did you know I met with Tucker?"

Brooke rolls her eyes. "You told me. Remember? Last night, via text?"

"Oh. Right." I nod, like I know what I'm talking about, but deep down, I'm a little confused. Still blown away by the fact that Tucker made an appointment with me yesterday, and how…pleasant it turned out, to sit and talk with him.

I'd felt such pride when he studied the photos of my cakes with awe. His compliments were the perfect balm to my bruised ego, because I can't help but feel a little bruised and beat up in Tucker's presence. He hurt me so badly all those years ago with his callous ways, how easily he broke up with me, and while the sting has definitely faded over the years, I still sort of hate him for what he did.

Though hate is such a strong word. One I don't like to use unless I really, really mean it. And when it comes to Tucker, I don't really hate him.

No way could I ever hate him…

"He was perfectly nice," I tell her when I see she's anxiously waiting for me to give her more details. "I thought it was sweet, how much he cares about his parents and their anniversary."

"So this meeting wasn't a ruse to spend time with you?" Brooke raises her brows.

I shake my head. "No, not at all. He is clearly planning a party for his parents' fortieth wedding anniversary, and somehow he's the one stuck with getting the cake."

"I would bet big money he requested that job," Brooke says dryly.

"Maybe." I shrug. Take a sip of my wine. "Maybe not."

He probably did. He seemed very eager to get my phone number. I never did send him any renderings of the possible cake, but I did work on it this morning.

And this afternoon.

Yet it's still not right, and now I'm frustrated. When Brooke texted me earlier asking if she could come over with a bottle of wine, I practically begged her to get here ASAP.

I needed the wine. And the company.

"You are being way too nonchalant about this entire thing," Brooke accuses and her words trigger something inside of me buried deep.

Making me explode.

"*Nonchalant?* Tell me how I should act then. Should I slobber all over him and beg him to take me back?" I toss out, my voice edged with anger.

Now it's Brooke's turn to blink at me. "Well…no. Definitely not."

"Okay. So should I be cold and rude to him, and tell him to stay the hell out of my life?" I ask.

"Well…no. You probably shouldn't do that either."

"Right. So meeting with him like we're two logical adults about to do business with each other is the way I should handle it, am I right?" When she nods mutely, I smile in triumph. "Then quit giving me shit over this. I don't know how else to handle Tucker."

"If he looks as good in person as he does on the TV screen, then I can think of a few extra special ways you could handle Tucker," Brooke says sarcastically, waggling her eyebrows at me.

"Please. He's not interested in me that way." I shake my head, perking up when I hear a notification. I move closer to the sink, where I left my phone, and pick it up to see I have a text.

From Tucker.

Like he could feel me talking about him. Thinking about him.

How's the cake design coming?

I should've texted him first and given an update. Now I feel unprofessional.

I should have something for you to look at by tomorrow! Sorry I didn't text anything last night.

I chew on my lip, thinking up the right thing to say.

I've been busy.

Lame, but he'll probably buy it.

No problem, he says seconds later. **Can't wait to see what you come up with.**

The pressure is on. I do *not* want to disappoint him.

Tucker sends me another text.

It was great seeing you yesterday.

I press my lips together to keep my smile contained, ignoring the flurry of butterflies set off by reading his simple words.

Deciding to keep it strictly professional, I compose the most business-like text I can think of.

I'm glad I could be of assistance for your parents' party.

Aw come on Maise. We're old friends. You can be friendlier than that.

I'm being perfectly friendly, I shoot back.

He sends me a laughing/crying face emoji in response.

"Who are you texting?"

My head shoots up, my eyes wide as I stare at my sister. "Um, no one."

"Liar." Brooke moves closer, craning her head to try and see my phone screen, but I never did type in Tucker's name, so just his number appears. "Who is it?"

"I'll never tell," I say, running around the kitchen so I'm standing on the other side of the island.

"It's Tucker, isn't it?" Brooke sounds triumphant and again I'm consumed with the need to smack her. What's up with my violent feelings toward my sister tonight?

My phone buzzes and I glance down.

Not friendly enough for me.

He adds a winking emoji face to the text.

Okay. It feels like he's flirting with me. And I want to…

Flirt back.

How friendly are you wanting me?

I send the text before I can overthink it.

"Maisey!" My sister is yelling at me, something she rarely does. "Who are you talking to?"

"Fine, it's Tucker," I say with a sigh, waiting on his response. I'm a jumble of nerves, anticipation coursing through my veins as I wait.

And wait and wait.

"Are you going to hook up with him while he's here?" Brooke asks, sounding downright hopeful.

"I don't plan on it," I tell her, because that's the absolute truth.

But maybe…it wouldn't be such a bad idea?

Okay, clearly I've lost my mind.

Another buzz and I read his response, unable to contain the smile that spreads across my face.

As friendly as you want to be pretty girl

Oh. *Swoon.* He used to call me that all the time when we were together. Pretty girl. I should be offended. I'm a grown woman, not some silly little teenage girl who hangs on Tucker McCloud's every word.

Yet I can't help the giddy feeling deep inside me at him calling me that. At the idea of us…what? Messing around? Having a fling? Getting back together?

We can't get back together. This is all temporary. He'll leave eventually. My home is here. His is in San Francisco. He has this entirely different life, a life that doesn't come close to resembling mine, which means we'd never work. And he knows it.

I know it too.

Another text from Tucker appears.

Have you had dinner yet?

No.

Want to have dinner with me?

I contemplate his invitation, ignoring Brooke, who's going on about reuniting with old loves and how it can work out no matter what, but she and Brody are different. Brody was willing to change his entire life for her to make it work.

Tucker doesn't even have that option. He's a professional football player. Why would he toss away his career to move back to his hometown to what? Hang out with me? There are no guarantees in life, meaning there's no guarantee we'd work. I can't imagine he'd throw his entire life and career away to try one more time with me.

I wouldn't want him to do that. It's asking for too much.

Brooke is suddenly standing right next to me, reading over my conversation with Tucker. "You should say yes. Go to dinner with him," she encourages gently and I send her a worried look.

"Really?" I almost want her to tell me not to do it. So I can blame someone else on my decision.

Deep down, though, I want to go to dinner with him. I want to catch up, relive old memories, laugh and talk about people we used to know in school. I want to hear what his life is like since he started playing for the NFL, and I want to know if he's truly happy or not. I want to know all the things that make Tucker who he is now.

My phone rings, startling us both, and we start to laugh.

"Guess he's anxious to know your answer," Brooke says when she sees his number flash on the screen.

The moment I answer his call, Tucker's deep voice is right there, murmuring into my ear, making me shiver. "Come on, Maise. Go to dinner with me."

"All right," I say, my voice soft as I turn my back on Brooke.

I don't want her looking at me while I'm talking to Tucker. This moment, this short conversation feels too big, too intimate, to share it with anyone else but the two of us.

"Really? You want to?" He sounds surprised.

And excited.

I start to laugh all over again. "Yes, I really want to."

"Can I come pick you up in, say, an hour?"

"That sounds perfect."

Chapter Six

Tucker

I take the fastest shower known to man the moment I end the call with Maisey. I shave my face, wash my hair, then actually blow that shit dry because I want to look perfect for this girl tonight.

The girl who used to be *my* girl.

I change my shirt three times until I get it right and end up annoyed with myself. Slap on some cologne and immediately think I put on too much, but there's nothing I can do about it now. Ignore the phone calls that come first from Georgia, then from Stella, then from Georgia one more time, who ends up leaving me a voicemail.

My sisters are complete pains in my ass, but what else is new?

I listen to the voicemail and she's asking about the cake, and the party, and the costume idea, and she sounds annoyed by the entire thing.

Deleting her voicemail, I tell myself I'll call her tomorrow.

I finish getting ready way faster than I thought and to help kill time, I start pacing my hotel room, my gaze snagging on the window and the gorgeous lake view. There are still a few boats on the water, and it makes me think I should borrow my brother's boat and take it out for the day.

Maybe I could take Maisey with me.

Pacing the hotel room only lasts for so long until I finally decide *fuck it* and leave the hotel, hop into my rental car, and haul ass over to Maisey's place. She texted me the address earlier, and when I pull up in front of the duplex, I find that it's in the older part of town. But it's been kept up nicely, with mature trees providing plenty of shade and a lush green lawn in the front. I'm fifteen minutes early from my "pick you up in an hour" promise, but I don't care.

I'm too anxious to get this night started.

The door swings open before I can even knock and Maisey is standing there in a pretty white sundress that accentuates her golden skin, her lips curved in a welcoming smile. "You're early."

"Yet you're ready," I say, letting my gaze linger.

Damn, she's pretty.

She laughs and pulls the door shut behind her, not even giving me a glimpse of what's inside. I'm sort of disappointed, considering I'm curious about everything that makes up today's Maisey. I want to see where she lives, where she eats, where she sleeps.

Yeah, the perv buried deep inside of me definitely wants to see her bed.

"I'm ready because I'm starving," she says as she locks her front door.

"Where do you want to eat?" I ask as we start down the walkway, headed toward my rental car.

"Wherever you want to go," she says with a slight shrug. The movement causes me to zero in on her slender shoulders, and I'm hit with the sudden urge to kiss them.

Slow your roll, McCloud. At least get the woman some dinner first.

"Is that one steak place still open?" I ask.

"The place where you took me for winter formal? Yeah, it is," she says with a wistful smile.

Winter Formal. My senior year, her junior year. Where I thought I was going to get lucky and finally, *finally* have sex with the girl I was in love with.

Instead, Maisey had one too many beers—and she only had two— and proceeded to throw up for the rest of the night. Such a lightweight.

"You're remembering when I threw up, huh?" she says, amusement filling her tone.

I hit the unlock button on the keyless remote and open the passenger side door for her. "I am, actually."

"Talk about a disastrous end to a fun night." She gets into the car, smiling up at me as I'm about to shut the door for her. "I still don't really like beer."

"You don't say." My voice is sarcastic, making her laugh.

I like this, I think as I jog around the front of the car and open the door, slipping into the driver's seat. I like that we have a past, a shared history that we can reminisce about. I don't want to focus on our breakup, but it's definitely fun to talk about the good times.

Maisey and I? We shared a lot of good times together.

"I didn't throw up at my senior prom," she tells me as I start the car.

"Who'd you go with?" I ask, my voice tight. Shit.

Clearly I need to relax.

"Jimmy Pearce." She smiles. "We had a lot of fun."

White hot jealousy rips through me and I'm tempted to go find stupid Jimmy Pearce and tear his heart out of his chest.

Dramatic much?

"We were just friends, though," she continues, staring out the passenger side window as I start driving through her neighborhood, headed for the steakhouse. "His girlfriend had a track meet the same day—it was the state finals. No way could she skip out on that to go to a stupid prom."

The relief that floods me at hearing the word girlfriend is huge. And makes me feel stupid. Why should I be jealous of her senior prom date, considering I'm the one who broke up with her in the first place?

"Did she win any events?" I ask.

"She did." Her smile is faint and I try to concentrate on the road and not stare at her, but it's difficult. "And she went to college on a track scholarship. Almost a full ride. You remember Kaya Owen?"

"I do." Cute. Long legs. Smart. Fast. "So. You didn't have a, uh, boyfriend your senior year?"

"No, I didn't. I decided I wanted to be free my last year in school. Didn't want anyone to tie me down." She glances over at me, her gaze contemplative. "You have any serious girlfriends these last few years?"

"Serious? Nah." I shake my head. "I don't have time for anything serious." During college, I wasn't looking for anything serious. I could get any girl I wanted, any time I wanted her. I sound like I'm bragging, but it's true.

"I figured you'd be married by now," she says.

"Funny, I thought the same thing about you."

I worried about it off and on, especially the last couple of years. Maybe it's because so many people we went to high school with started posting wedding pics on Instagram and Facebook. Or baby announcements. There've been a couple of divorces already, but I think that's pretty common.

"I've been concentrating on building my business," she tells me. "And there aren't a lot of eligible bachelors here in Cunningham Falls. Most of the good ones have already been snapped up."

"Your cakes are truly beautiful, Maise," I tell her, hoping she hears the sincerity in my voice. I mean every word I say. I almost feel proud of her success, like I even had a hand in it, which I most definitely did not.

But still. That's my first love, my high school sweetheart who can create such beauty. It's pretty freaking amazing.

"Thank you." Her voice is soft and I chance a quick glance at her to find she's watching me. "That means a lot, coming from you."

"Really?" Why should she care about my opinion? I'm just the teenage jackass who broke her heart.

She nods. "I've always cared about what you thought about me, even when I was mad at you. And I've been mad at you for a while." We both laugh, though it dies quick. "It's kind of weird, being here with you tonight."

My stomach twists with nerves. "Weird in a bad way, or weird in a good way?"

"Definitely in a good way." She tucks her hair behind her ear, exposing the tiny pearl dotting her lobe. "It'll be nice, catching up over dinner. Don't you think?"

"Sure," I say distractedly as I turn onto the main street that cuts through the busy downtown.

I'm not only looking forward to catching up on all those years we've lost, I also just want to spend time with her.

Looking at her.

Listening to her voice.

Fighting the urge to touch her.

Dreaming about her naked.

In my bed.

Maybe, just maybe she'll let my dreams come true tonight.

Chapter Seven

Maisey

It's so strange, how you can spend time with a person after not seeing him for years, and it's like we were never apart.

That's how it feels tonight with Tucker, sitting at the nicest restaurant in town, enjoying our drinks, our appetizers, me listening with rapt attention to Tucker's stories about his experiences with the NFL. He's played for three different teams, dealt with all sorts of personalities, and he's a master storyteller.

I can envision these men he's talking about—how one of them threw a major tantrum after every game, whether they lost or won. Another would always seek out the kindest looking older woman in the crowd, tell her she reminded him of the grandmother he'd lost, and give her a signed team jersey.

The tantrum story made me laugh. The grandma story made me a little emotional, and I had to force myself to not start crying like a baby.

And Tucker? He just plain makes me happy.

"Enough about me," he says once our server takes our salad plates away. I'm already stuffed, and we haven't even started on the main course yet. "Tell me about you. What have you been doing with yourself since high school? Did you go to college? How did you start making cakes? I don't remember you baking much when we were together."

My heart clenches at thinking of us together, and me never baking. The only thing I remember making with Tucker were those Halloween-themed sugar cookies that you throw on a baking sheet and cook for ten minutes. And those definitely don't count.

"I was a little lost after high school. I wasn't sure what I wanted to do, and I was working at the market. You know, the one with the donuts?"

He nods, somehow looking hungry even though we've already eaten so much food. "I dreamed of those donuts every so often over the years. They're something you can't ever forget."

Tucker is so freaking dramatic sometimes, I think with a giggle. "Yeah, well, I started frosting the donuts. And I was having so much fun, I'll have to show you my photos sometime. Anyway, my ideas were creative enough that they moved me to the cake section of the bakery, and I started decorating them. You know, the standard birthday cakes with white frosting and pink roses in the corners?" When Tucker nods, I continue. "When I got bored with that, then I graduated to wedding cakes, though the market didn't do too many of those. Every time I got to work on one though, I was always so happy. I just let my creative juices flow and came up with some pretty awesome stuff."

"That's cool," he says with a nod, leaning back in his chair, and I can't help but admire him.

Did I mention how handsome he looks tonight? Dark rinse jeans, white button-down shirt with the sleeves rolled up, revealing those strong, muscular forearms. His light brown hair is extra messy tonight, flopping over his forehead. My fingers itch to push it back, test the silky softness.

I can't stop staring at him.

And for some reason, it seems he can't stop staring at me either.

"I started thinking I wanted to go to culinary school, but there wasn't one close enough, and they were all so expensive. I took some business courses at the local community college, but I barely lasted there two years. It was expensive, and I'd rather spend my time working and making money." I shrug, hating how inadequate I suddenly feel. It has nothing to do with Tucker either. This is my own problem to deal with. A problem that's absolutely ridiculous, considering I am a business owner, and a decently successful one at that.

"Not all of us are meant to go on to college," he observes.

"I wish I had though," I say with a sigh, bringing my wineglass to my lips and drinking the last sip. "That's my one regret."

He raises a brow. "Your one regret is that you didn't go to college?"

I nod, feeling helpless. "I was so jealous of everyone leaving, of everyone doing something with their lives, and getting out of Cunningham Falls. Yet here I am, stuck in the same town I grew up in, never really moving ahead."

"Are you serious right now?" Tucker's voice is sharp and he leans forward, his intense gaze locking with mine. "You're describing yourself like you're some sort of—*loser.*"

His words make me flinch. "I don't think I'm a loser."

"Then why say it like that? *'Oh, I stayed here. I've done nothing with my life. Wah wah.'*" He points a finger at me, his expression stern. "You're fucking amazing, Maise, and don't you forget it. You have your own business, you make your own hours, you bake cakes that look like masterpieces, and you're gorgeous. So what if you ended up staying in Cunningham Falls? Our hometown is beautiful, and it's become a thriving community, which only helps you and your business in the long run. There's no need for you to have a pity party, baby. You should be damn proud of yourself."

I blink at him, shocked by his mini rant. Shocked and a little bit...

Aroused.

I uncross and re-cross my legs, startled by the sudden ache there. Who knew Tucker defending me would be such a turn-on?

"You're right," I tell him, my voice faint. "I don't know why I was acting so pitiful just now. My life is pretty great."

"Hell, yeah, it is," he says firmly.

"I don't have anyone telling me what to do. Well, I do have the occasional bridezilla," I add, making him smile. "But they're fine. I know how to handle them."

"Because you're awesome," he says.

"Right." I'm smiling. I feel giddy. Light as air. "Because I'm awesome."

"You know what's my one regret?" he asks, swiftly changing the subject.

My smile fades. He looks so serious. And sincere. Terribly, horribly sincere. "What?" I whisper.

"That I broke up with you. That I gave up so easily on us." He blinks, appearing startled by his admission, and I secretly love that. He's leaving himself open to me. Raw and vulnerable. "That's my one regret over anything else, Maise. If I could go back in time and correct that mistake, I wouldn't even hesitate. Just to see where our lives would've taken us. Aren't you curious?"

"Curious about what?" I'm still whispering. This moment is...reverent. As if we're in church, confessing our secrets. Our sins.

And asking each other for forgiveness.

"What would've happened to us if we'd stayed together?" He reaches across the table and takes my hand, his thumb stroking across the top of it, making me shiver with awareness. God, I love it when he touches me.

I always have.

"I—I never gave it much thought," I say, my words stalling in my throat, and his lips curve in that knowing smile of his.

As in, he knows I'm full of crap.

"Really?" He lifts my hand and brings it to his lips, but he doesn't kiss me. He just holds my hand there, so I can feel his warm breath, his damp lips. "I don't believe you."

"I mean, fine. Yes, I thought about you when we first broke up and if we're being truthful tonight, I can admit that I was totally devastated." The pain that crosses his face at my words is worth the admission. "But after a while, I just..."

"You just what?"

"Gave up thinking about you," I say with a shrug. "Like you gave up on me."

Chapter Eight

Tucker

Maisey's words hang in the air, hover over the table, and I'm about to respond when our server chooses that moment to deliver our dinner. I drop Maisey's hand and smile up at the server as she sets our plates in front of us. When she finishes, she's gone in an instant, off to take care of another table.

"Looks delicious," Maisey says as she takes in her steak and baked potato.

The lack of emotion in her voice is obvious.

"Yeah, it does," I agree, though my appetite has left me.

I hate that she thinks I gave up on her. That wasn't the reason for the break up. I just believed...

Shit. I don't know what exactly I believed. I was eighteen and stupid. Headed for Texas A&M—my dream school—on a football scholarship. I felt like I was finally going places, that my life was going to take me on a different track.

And I didn't want Maisey sitting at home waiting for me, lonely and sad. I didn't want to hold her back. She deserved to be free.

So I cut her loose, believing the entire time that I was doing her a favor.

Instead, now I'm starting to think I just made the both of us miserable.

"I was an idiot for ending things," I say just as she starts cutting into her steak.

The knife she's holding clatters on her plate as she stares at me. "What did you just say?"

"I was an idiot," I repeat, hoping she realizes how fucking real I'm being with her right now. "I should've never broken up with you."

"Okay." She draws the word out, and I know she doesn't believe me. "But you still did it."

"I know. And that was stupid. I was eighteen, and so fucking dumb." I shake my head, never taking my eyes off her. I hope she knows. I hope she realizes every single word I'm saying is the absolute truth. "I hate that I hurt you."

"It was a long time ago—" she starts but I cut her off.

"Doesn't matter. I still hurt you, and it still hurts me, that I gave up on what we had. That I ruined it." Having her sitting across from me, beautiful and sweet and in pain, I know without a doubt she's the woman I've been looking for all my life.

Yet I threw her away.

"You didn't ruin anything. We probably wouldn't have lasted anyway," she says, so very matter of fact.

"But what if we had? We could still be together."

"Okay, so I'd be living with you in San Francisco and doing…what? Having your babies?"

The idea of her pregnant with my baby fills me with some unfamiliar, primal need. I'd like to see her body ripe with my child.

"I would've never become the independent businesswoman you just told me you admired," she continues.

True.

"We had to take our separate paths to become who we are today, right?" Her smile is genuine, though her eyes are still a little sad. "And that's okay. I'm happy with who I am. Aren't you happy?"

"I am." But I bet I'd be happier if she was back in my life.

For good.

* * * *

We leave the restaurant and the sun is long gone, the air carrying a slight chill. It's still early summer; we're not even midway through June but we haven't been hit with a brutal heat wave yet. I'm not surprised then when I catch Maisey shivering.

Perfect excuse for me to sling my arm around her shoulders and tuck her in close to me. "You look cold," I tell her, my mouth hovering close to her temple. I take a sniff, catching the floral scent of her shampoo, and my body goes on high alert.

I want her. No surprise.

"A little," she admits, snuggling in closer as we walk together toward my car. "Summer will be upon us soon enough. I bet by the Fourth of July I'll be complaining about how hot it is."

"Summer will be here officially next week," I remind her, surprised that I even know this.

"And wedding season is in full swing." She smiles up at me. "I've got one wedding this weekend, but next weekend is going to be insane, what with the two weddings and a 40th anniversary party."

"About that." I stop walking and so does she. "You're coming to my parents' party, right?"

"Oh. I didn't think I was invited." She blinks those big brown eyes up at me, and I'm tempted to devour her where she stands.

But I restrain myself.

"You're definitely invited," I say fiercely. "Plus it's a costume party."

She starts to laugh. "You got everyone to go along with that idea?"

"Yeah, when I told Georgia about the cake design and I suggested costumes, she totally went for it. We're all supposed to dress like we're in The Great Gatsby movie. The DiCaprio version," I explain to her as we start walking again.

Now Maisey is full blown laughing. "Oh, that ought to be funny, seeing you in your twenties' gear."

"Are you making fun of me?" I nudge her side.

"Maybe." She nudges me back. "Where am I going to find a costume? I don't have much time."

"You have over a week. And Amazon is an amazing thing," I suggest.

"Hmm. I do have a Prime membership," she says, pursing her lips. "Think I could find a costume there?"

"I know you can." That's where I already found mine.

"I'll have to check it out."

We come to a stop at my rental car and I reluctantly remove my arm from around her shoulders so I can open the door for her. "Will you be my date?"

She whirls around, frowning at me. "Date for what?"

"The anniversary party." I smile, suddenly feeling nervous. Like I'm a teenage kid again, asking my favorite girl to prom. "My parents would probably love that. To see us back together again."

I say the words and I can see the flicker of emotion in her gaze, the creases in her forehead as she frowns. Maybe I pushed too hard. I shouldn't have said that. I shouldn't assume anything. I'm walking on thin ice here.

And I don't want to screw this up. Not again.

"I'm sure they would," she murmurs just before she slides into the passenger seat. "Can I think about it? Before I give you my answer?"

My heart drops in my gut. There goes my chance at a goodnight kiss. "Sure," I say easily, just before I slam her car door. "Think about it all you want," I mutter under my breath. "You know where to find me."

Chapter Nine

Maisey

"…and so then I asked him if I could think about it first. Before I give him my answer," I finish, waiting for my older sister's reaction.

By the way she's gaping at me like I've just lost my mind, it's not a good one.

"He asked you to be his date at his parents' anniversary party, and you asked him if you could *think* about it first?" she asks incredulously.

We're at her flower shop, since we just met with a potential client looking for flowers and the cake for her wedding. It's such a bonus that we're a one-stop shop for both, but now our future client is gone and Brooke is being her usual self.

An interrogator.

I nod at her question, hating the dread that is filling me, making my stomach churn. "I shouldn't have said that?" I ask weakly.

"Uh, no." She's shaking her head, her disappointment clear. "Maise, it's Tucker. Your first love. Hell, I consider him your *only* love."

"Oh please. I can find more love. He's not the only fish in the sea," I remind her. God, I sound like our mother with that fish in the sea nonsense.

"Yeah, but for some reason, he seems to be the only fish for you," she stresses. "You haven't dated many guys beyond Tucker."

"I've dated lots of guys." I raise my chin, going for indignant, knowing deep down I'm exaggerated.

I've gone out with a few guys. Not what I would consider "lots."

"That's the key word. *Dated.* Nothing's ever stuck. Like, ever," Brooke says. "And I don't know if I'd use the word lots either, sister." I swear to God she's a mind reader. "More like…a few."

Damn it, she's right. About everything. Not that I'm going to admit it. "It doesn't matter," I say, waving a hand. "He's here temporarily. Soon he'll go back home to California and forget all about me."

"I thought a certain someone would go back home to California and forget all about me too, but that so didn't happen." Brooke holds up her hand and waves her fingers, her diamond engagement ring catching the light and nearly blinding me. "I think Tucker's realizing what he gave up. And I'm guessing he's interested in giving you another try."

I seriously hate how she just phrased that. "Maybe I'm *not* interested in giving him another try," I mutter, dropping my head so I can gaze at my hands, which are currently twisted together in my lap. Something I always do when I'm nervous.

"Then you should tell him," Brooke says, her voice firm. "Don't lead him on if you're not interested."

"Who said anything about Tucker wanting to give this—*us*—another try? Maybe he's just in it for a fling! He's probably just curious. See if there's still a spark between us or whatever," I say with a dismissive wave of my hand.

"Are you curious to see if there's still a spark?" Brooke asks cautiously.

Yes. I already know there's a spark. The energy crackles between us when we're together. And when we touch? It's like an electric shock every time he puts his hands on me. Imagine if he kissed me again. Actually…stripped me naked and did all of those wicked things I used to imagine when we were younger and I had no clue what to do.

I swallow hard and lift my head, my gaze locking with Brooke's. "There's still a spark."

Her smug smile is annoying.

"Of course, there's a spark," I say irritably. "We always had chemistry. Isn't that normal?"

"No, not really."

I think of Brooke's words the entire way home. It's not normal for a couple who were together as teens to still have chemistry. I guess I should know that. A relationship, especially one in high school, usually runs its course. As in, when it's over, it's over.

And teenage relationships usually end spectacularly. Dramatically.

There was no drama between Tucker and me. Everything was fine until he got that letter of acceptance from his dream college. He started to withdraw, but I figured it was just…senior blues or something. Knowing that in a few short months, he'd be thrust out into the world all on his own.

I know the thought terrified me.

But then one day, he came to school, pulled me aside, and gently broke up with me. He didn't even seem that upset. No, more like he was quiet, emotionless. He apologized, swore it had nothing to do with me.

It was all on him.

I've had a pretty decent life so far. No major catastrophes. No horrible losses. There have been a few hurdles as my business has grown, but nothing I can't eventually tackle. I consider myself lucky. Blessed.

The worst thing that's ever happened to me so far is Tucker ending our relationship. While he gave his reasons, it still felt abrupt.

I had no closure. One moment he was there, and the next he was gone. Vanished. Out of my life for good. I didn't even go to the graduation ceremony that year, and I hadn't missed one of those since my eighth grade year. But I couldn't bear the thought of watching him receive his diploma, seeing him celebrate with his family and friends, knowing that he would soon leave Cunningham Falls forever.

It hurt too much.

Did he feel the same? Was the end of our relationship the worst thing he ever experienced? He's led a fuller life than me, only because of his experiences. And he said he had regret over breaking up with me. He actually said if he could go back and change that moment, he would without hesitation. That threw me, because I've often wondered what would've happened if we'd stayed together.

Then he goes and says the same thing.

Why, after all these years, does he walk back into my life and turn it completely upside down? Am I giving him too much power? Or did he have that power all along?

Maybe he's just looking for closure.

Maybe I'm just looking for closure too.

I'm tempted to bang my head against the steering wheel. It's all so freaking confusing. I don't know how I feel about Tucker. Worse, I don't know how I *should* feel.

All I know is that I still enjoy spending time with him. I want to see him again. Yes, I'm curious. Yes, maybe I'm looking for closure.

And maybe I'm looking for the chance to kiss him one more time. Just to see if it's as good as I remembered.

I'm entering the kitchen from the garage, setting my purse on the counter when I receive a text. No surprise, it's from Tucker. I must admit that I get a tiny thrill seeing his name flash on my phone screen.

You're leaving me hanging :)

Smiling, I try to come up with the proper, flirtatious response. Because screw it. I'm going to flirt with Tucker. I'm going to spend as much time with him as possible before he leaves for California. I can keep my heart out of this, right? Just two old friends rekindling the fun part of their relationship.

I accept your invitation, is what I finally settle on saying.

He responds without hesitation.

Better round up a proper costume. Gatsby themed, don't forget.

I'm still smiling when I send him my reply.

How could I forget? Can't wait!

Then I proceed to search the web for a sexy Gatsby costume for the rest of the evening.

Chapter Ten

Tucker

I convinced Hunter to let me use his boat, and this is how I end up torturing myself on a sunny Thursday with Maisey.

She's wearing a bikini.

It's red.

And tiny.

It shows off every curve she's got, and she's got plenty. The swell of her breasts, her flaring hips, her perfect ass. Long legs and sexy shoulders and with her dark hair up in that high ponytail, I catch glimpses of her kissable neck all afternoon as we cruise around the lake and that's all I can think about.

Kissing that neck.

Sliding my hand inside the scrap of red fabric to see if her nipples are hard.

Or sliding my hand into the back of her bikini bottoms so I can cup that perfect ass.

Better yet, sliding my hand into the front of her bikini bottoms so I can dip my fingers—

"Holy shit!" I scream when Maisey splashes cold water in my face.

Yeah. I screamed like a little baby just now when she splashed me, but holy *hell* that water is freezing. My face and chest are currently dripping with snow melt straight off the mountain and despite the intense afternoon sun beating down on me, I'm shivering.

Her laughter rings, warming me up from the inside. I always did like her laugh. She doesn't hold back, just lets it rip, and despite the goosebumps and the water dripping from the tip of my nose, I'm smiling.

"Gotcha," she says, flicking her fingers at me, raining little droplets of water all over my arm, a silly grin on her face.

We're near the shoreline, the motor off and the boat rocking gently with the waves created by the water skiers nearby. The lake isn't so crowded with tourists since we're still early in the season but after July Fourth, the water will be packed until Labor Day.

Meaning we picked a perfect day to be on the lake.

I'm beginning to realize that any day spent with this woman is perfect.

Eyeing Maisey, my gaze lingers on the way her body is still draped over the edge of the boat. That's how she was able to splash me with water. How I didn't notice her dangling over the edge is beyond me.

All I can do now is stare at her ass, the way the rounded cheeks peek out a little, tempting me to smack her right there. Just a light smack, to shock her, make her yelp. What would she do? Would she hate it?

Maybe she'd like it...

"Your brother's boat is amazing," she says, rising to her feet and sauntering toward me. She braces herself when the boat rocks extra hard and I almost reach for her before she rights herself. "Thank you for taking me out."

"Thank you for splashing me," I tell her solemnly, making her smile.

"You needed it. You were so serious only a few minutes ago, trying to maneuver this thing." She shakes her head, rests her hands on her hips. "Please tell me we'll hang out here for a little bit before we head back to the dock."

"Sure." I dropped the anchor when we first got here, and I planned on busting a few drinks out of the ice chest I brought with us. Maisey was in charge of snacks, and even though I ate lunch only an hour ago, my stomach is growling in anticipation of what she might have in her bag. "Thirsty?"

"Yes." She nods.

I flip open the top of the blue ice chest and contemplate the selection. "I have Coke, Water, one 7-Up, a couple of beers, and two

Orange Crushes."

She wrinkles her nose when my gaze meets hers. "Quite the variety."

"I picked everything from Hunter's refrigerator." My brother has a fridge in the garage where they keep extra stuff and all the drinks.

"I'll take an Orange Crush, please," Maisey says primly and I dig into the ice, pull the cold can out, and hand it to her, our fingers brushing.

Our touch hot despite the ice.

"Thank you," she murmurs, cracking open the can.

"You still like them," I tell her as she takes a sip.

"I still like what?"

"Orange Crushes. You used to always drink them when…" *We were together,* I say silently.

"I don't drink them like I used to." She takes another sip, a hum of satisfaction sounding low in her throat. My skin goes tight at the sound. "I've pretty much given up soda these last couple of years."

"I brought the Orange Crush for you," I admit as I grab a beer—the only one I'll drink while we're out on the boat—and twist the cap off. "I saw it in Hunter's fridge and had to throw it in there. Just in case."

"Just in case what?"

"Just in case you still drank them." The beer feels good on my dry throat and I drain almost half of it, like I need the liquid courage to continue with my plan.

My plan to get my hands on Maisey in that fucking bikini.

From the moment I stopped by her house to pick her up, driving Hunter's truck with the boat towed behind it, she threw me. Looking cute and so painfully young in her cutoff jean shorts and a white tank top, the bright red straps of her swimsuit top curved around her neck. Seeing her with no makeup on her pretty face and her hair in that ponytail took me right back. To when we were young and in love and blind to the future.

We were living in the here and now.

I envy my younger self. When I didn't care, when all I could focus on was football and school and my girlfriend. My friends and my family and my beat-up truck I bought with the money I'd saved up. How proud I was to drive around town in that truck with my girl sitting at my side, my hand on her thigh, her head on my shoulder.

I am nothing like the kid I was. And I'm filled with the sudden urge to reclaim my old self.

Even if it's just for a little bit.

"You want something to eat?" she asks and my earlier hungry thoughts are gone, replaced by a need to do something fun.

Something spontaneous.

"Let's jump in the water," I say as I set the beer in the cupholder by the driver's seat.

"It'll be cold," Maisey warns, setting her soda can in the other cupholder.

"Once we jump in, it'll be fine," I say with a confidence I don't necessarily feel.

She's right. That water will be damn cold. It'll be a shock to my system. Just her splashing me in the face shook me completely.

I grab hold of her hand and help her join me on the tiny deck at the back of the boat. We stand there, our weight tipping the boat, our gazes meeting for a brief moment before her lips part and she says, "We'll jump on three."

"One," I say, squeezing her hand.

"Two," she adds, blowing out a harsh breath.

"Three!" we both scream at the same time as we jump into the lake.

The icy temperature takes my breath away as I plunge into the water, my fingers still curled around Maisey's. We sink and sink, me taking her along for the ride since my weight is pulling her down. And then I'm dragging her back up, our feet kicking, our heads popping above the water simultaneously, both of us gasping for air.

"Oh my God!" she's yelling, pushing the tangle of wet hair away from her face. "It is. So. Cold!"

I pull her to me so our bodies collide, our feet churning around each other, our chests bumping. She sucks in a breath, her gaze meeting mine, her expression open. Tempting.

Leaning in, I give her a quick kiss, her lips warm despite the temperature.

When I pull away, she's blinking up at me, her lips parted, our legs still moving, keeping us in place. "Why did you do that?"

"I wanted to." I touch her cheek, her skin frigid, though I can still feel the warmth lingering just below the surface. "I want to do so much more than kiss you, Maise."

"Oh." She's still blinking at me, appearing confused, and at first, I wonder if I made a mistake.

But then she's letting go of my hand, her arms circling around my neck, her body snug against mine. A perfect fit. I slip my arm about her waist, pinning her to me, knowing we only have a few seconds before we'll start sinking and suddenly her mouth is there.

On mine.

Kissing me.

I return the kiss with all the pent-up hunger I've felt for her since the moment I saw her at the grocery store. Though it goes further than that. All of this hunger and need coursing through my body goes back years. To that last moment I had with her, in the cab of my trunk the night before I broke up with her.

When I kissed her freely because she was mine.

That word is running through my brain right now as our lips part and our tongues tangle.

Mine.

It repeats, keeps the rhythm of my heartbeat as I devour her.

Mine.

Mine.

Mine.

I take the kiss deeper and she wraps her legs around my waist, anchoring herself to me. I start to go under, struggling to keep above water without letting go of her, and when we break the kiss, she's laughing.

"I don't want to drown you," she murmurs, her face so close I can see the water droplets clinging to her eyelashes. The tiny scar on the left side of her chin. The rosy lushness of her mouth.

I want to taste that mouth again. I want to feel her mouth on my skin.

I want to feel her everywhere.

"Let's get back on the boat," I suggest, reluctantly loosening my hold on her.

"What are we going to do once we get back on the boat?" Her eyebrows shoot up, her expression questioning.

"Whatever you want me to do," I answer, my voice full of promise.

Chapter Eleven

Maisey

We scramble back onto the boat, both of us breathless and laughing, my entire body tingling, but not from the water.

No, my body is tingling from Tucker's kiss. From his touch. A few stolen moments in the lake and my body is aching for more. More of Tucker's hands, more of Tucker's lips, more of Tucker's skin…

My laughter dies. He's standing in front of me now, dripping wet, rivulets of water streaming down his wide chest, making my mouth run dry as I stare at him. He's so—*large*. Tall and broad and packed tightly with muscle. The lightest bit of dark hair curls between his pecs and his stomach is a literal washboard. Ab-tacular. Ab-tastic.

All the silly words describing his perfect abs don't measure up to actually seeing them up close. In the flesh. My fingers literally itch to touch him there.

I curl my fingers into fists instead, telling myself I need to remain in control.

"You're looking at me like you want to jump me," he says, his amused voice breaking the sudden tension that formed between us.

I burst out laughing because he's not telling lies. I do want to jump him. "You're looking at me in the same way."

He smiles. Pushes his wet hair away from his forehead, his biceps bulging. His body is so much more…delicious than it was when we were younger. He was always built as a teen, but he wasn't quite so big and masculine and dominating.

"I'm trying to control myself," he says, his voice low and gruff.

"Me too," I murmur.

Tucker takes a step toward me. "Not like I'm going to do anything to you here on a boat in the middle of the afternoon."

I mock pout. "That's too bad."

He chuckles, and the sound is devastatingly sexy. "You want me to strip you naked and have my way with you right now? So if anyone drives by, they could see us?"

Everything inside of me goes liquid at the promise in his words, his voice, his eyes. *Yes, yes, YES!* I want to shout, but I don't. "Maybe," I say with a little shrug.

His smile turns wicked and then he's right in front of me, his hands on my waist, his fingers burning into my bare skin. I had no idea I missed his touch so badly until I had his hands on me once again.

Now I'm not sure how I'll ever survive without him.

"You've been driving me crazy since the moment you stepped on this boat and took your clothes off," he says, his head bent close to mine as he watches his hands slide along my waist. "Wearing a swimsuit like that."

He sounds annoyed. Frustrated. And I love it. "Oh, this little thing?" I ask innocently.

"You wore it on purpose," he accuses, but he doesn't sound angry.

He sounds like he's barely in control of himself.

"You always did like me in red," I remind him. It was the color of my dress to winter formal. That night, he couldn't stop staring at me. Told me again and again how beautiful I looked.

I still have the corsage he gave me, dried out and stashed in a box of collectibles I keep in my spare bedroom closet.

"I definitely like you in this," he says, his fingers toying with the ties on my hips. "One tug on each side and your bottoms would fall off."

He slips his fingers beneath the fabric ties. They brush against my skin and I step closer, wishing he really would tug them off. I want to be bared to him. Open to him. I have nothing to hide with Tucker. He walks back into my life so easily, like he was never gone. And I want to accept him with open arms.

There are no warnings, no caution. I just…

I want.

Him.

"I have another regret, you know," he says, his voice casual, like there's nothing unusual about him trying to take off my bikini bottoms.

My skin is on fire. My nipples are hard, and not from the various temperatures I've put my body through in the last ten minutes. No, it's all Tucker's fault. In fact, I can barely speak, and I have to clear my throat before I croak, "What's your other regret?"

"That we never had sex," he says, his gaze meeting mine. "That we weren't each other's first."

My heart squeezes. I didn't realize how much I regret that fact until he just said it. "I always thought you would be," I admit.

"Same. I did too." The sadness is there, tingeing his voice, but his lips curve into a slow smile. "We did a lot of other fun things though."

Memories flood me. Fumbling hands removing clothes in the cab of his old truck. His fingers between my legs. A couple of pillows, a pile of blankets, and the two of us naked on a hot summer night, messing around, me too scared to go all the way, but perfectly willing to do everything else.

"Yeah, we did," I agree, my voice soft, a gasp escaping me when he grabs hold of my waist and picks me up with ease, bringing me with him as he settles on one of the bench seats at the front of the boat.

I straddle his hips, my hands resting on his smooth, hard shoulders, our faces close. I can feel his warm breath, the swell of his erection between my legs, and my eyes go wide when I realize our scandalous position.

At the front of the boat.

"You weren't lying when you said everyone could see us," I tell him, squeezing his shoulders.

"It's the most comfortable spot." His hands rest on my hips, fingers playing with my bikini bottom ties once more. "I'm a big guy."

"I can see that." And feel it. I mean, I've seen him naked before, but that was a long time ago. Memories fade and all that.

He slides his hands up my back. "I'm trying to use restraint."

"Why?" I sound incredulous, and that's because I *am* incredulous. There's no point in holding back. We're adults. We should just go for it.

"Something about anticipation. It's a killer, yet it's also *so* fucking good." He brushes his lips with mine, the touch whisper soft, making me sigh. "Now that I've got you back in my arms, I want to make this moment last."

"You want to torture us," I whisper, my lips moving against his when I speak.

"Absolutely." His fingers curl around my damp ponytail, tugging gently, and then his mouth settles on mine for three, four, ten heartbeats. Just our mouths touching, sharing the same air. Our bodies wrapped tight, as if we're trying to crawl inside each other's skin.

He whispers my name just before he deepens the kiss and I am lost. Lost to the sensation of his lips molded to mine. Drowning in his taste when his tongue slides inside my mouth, searching, seeking my tongue. He groans, I can feel the sound rumble in his chest, and I slide my hand down until it rests over his rapidly beating heart.

My heart is beating just as fast.

We kiss and kiss, the rhythmic rocking of the boat causing our bodies to rock together, driving me crazy. We keep our clothes on, but that's not saying much, considering we're wearing so little. My hands roam all over his shoulders and chest, drift across his perfect stomach, making the muscles contract. I explore as much as I can and so does he, his touch making me shiver.

Making me whimper.

Making me burn.

Our lips never part. I could kiss him forever, despite the sting of the sun on my skin. The roar of the boats as they pass us by. The loud music as a pontoon boat settles on the shore not too far from where we are.

"Get a room!" someone yells over the music and Tucker tears his mouth from mine, pushes me off his lap as gently as a push can possibly be, and rises to his feet to give the offending pontoon boat and its passengers a one-finger salute.

"Wait a minute!" another male voice yells, causing Tucker to go still. "Aren't you that football player? Tucker McCloud?"

It's almost comical, how his erection deflates when the guy asks him that question and Tucker sends me a pleading look. "The fans are about to descend."

"That's okay. Let them," I say, glancing down at myself to ensure no pink parts are inadvertently on display.

Within minutes the pontoon boat is right beside us and Tucker is joining them, surrounded by a bunch of guys who look young, but not too young. Most likely they're in college. They have a few women with them, all of them staring at Tucker with rapt attention and I can't help the stab of jealousy that pierces me when I see them ogling him.

But then Tucker calls, "Hey, babe, get on this boat and join us," and a surge of pride fills me at him calling me "babe."

Silly, I know.

I step onto the boat and someone shoves a cold water bottle in my hand and asks me if I want a burger. I'm suddenly ravenous—kissing Tucker must burn a lot of calories—and I agree to a cheeseburger, as does Tucker.

We spend the next hour with them, eating an early dinner, the men asking Tucker all sorts of questions, the ladies wanting photos with Tucker so they can post on Instagram or Snapchat or whatever.

I just sit there quietly, soaking up the sun, the breeze off the lake, the camaraderie, the way Tucker glances at me every once in a while, like he wants to ensure I'm still there. He smiles. He winks. He even mouths "Sorry," but I don't mind.

We're together. And I get to see him in his "I'm a celebrity" element, and it's an eye-opening moment. He's accomplished so much in a short amount of time, and these complete strangers are in total awe of his presence. They want a tiny piece of him, an experience they can share with their friends and family, so they can boast that they met the famous football player, Tucker McCloud.

Yet I know the *real* Tucker McCloud. The man behind the myth, the stories, the celebrity. I knew the boy he once was, and I loved him with all of my heart.

If given the chance, I could love him again. Even more fiercely this time.

The realization makes me want to cry.

Chapter Twelve

Tucker

Once we drop off Hunter's truck and boat and we get back into my rental car, I convince Maisey to come back with me to my hotel.

"The shower is amazing," I tell her, and I can see she's nibbling on her lower lip like she does when she's unsure. Funny how some things don't change. "The water pressure feels like a massage, swear to God. And the bathroom comes with extra soft terry cloth robes."

"Are you telling me you've wrapped that big body of yours into an extra soft terry cloth robe?" Maisey asks, clearly amused.

"No," I say slowly, reaching across the console to grab hold of her hand and squeeze it. "But I can definitely imagine you wearing the robe."

Her cheeks flush pink—or maybe they were already pink, since she got a lot of sun today. "You just want to get me into your bed."

Yeah. There's no denying that. But I also don't want the day to end. The sun has almost set, and I'm worn out, yet I want to keep going. I like the idea of taking a long shower and then crawling into bed. Naked.

With Maisey.

I decide to go with the honest approach.

"Fine, you're right," I admit. "I do want to get you in my bed."

She remains quiet for a while, and I continue driving, though a little slower than usual. We're still at the point where she can give me her answer and I can turn right and head back to my hotel.

Or I could turn left and go back to her place.

"Let's go to the hotel," she finally says and I'm tempted to pump my fist in victory.

But I don't.

With a lead foot I get us to the hotel in record time, dropping the keys and a twenty dollar bill in the valet's hand so he can park my car. I grab hold of Maisey's straw basket full of our mostly uneaten snacks and our towels, and I sling it over my shoulder, then take her hand and lead her inside.

We are windblown and sunburnt and I've never felt more alive. This has been the best day since I don't know when. And it's all thanks to Maisey.

She's quiet as we ride in the elevator to the top floor, and I wonder if she's tired. When we enter the room, I offer her the shower first, and she gladly takes it. I sit on the edge of the bed and suffer in silence as I listen to the water run, imagining her standing under the warm spray, naked and glistening.

Fuck.

Within fifteen minutes she's exiting the bathroom, wrapped up in that white terrycloth robe. It's a little big so the collar puffs up around her face and I stand, going to her so I can push aside the front of the robe and check out her skin.

"You got a little too much sun," I say, sounding like my mama when I tsk under my breath. Her chest is tinged red. More like pink, and it looks painful to the touch.

"It's not so bad. I think it looks worse than it feels. I brought some aloe and I already smoothed some on." She knocks my hand away and steps back, her expression exhausted. "I think I'll lay down while you take your shower."

Grabbing her hand, I reel her back in and drop a kiss to her forehead. "I won't be long."

I keep the water cool because I'm a little burnt too, and I wash myself quick, getting the lake water off me. I'm eager to get back to Maisey, to undo the belt on her robe and see if she's naked underneath.

I have a feeling she is.

After wrapping the towel around my waist and running my fingers through my hair, I swing the bathroom door open to see her lying on the bed, fast asleep. I've totally missed my chance.

There will be no naked exploration with Maisey tonight.

The girl is completely sacked out.

* * * *

I'm having the best dream.

Long, soft hair tickles across my chest. Warm, damp lips on my skin, a wet tongue flicking my nipple and I press my lips together, containing the moan desperate to escape.

My body goes tight, anticipation flowing through my veins as I wait for her next tentative touch. Gentle fingers caress my skin, skimming across my stomach, hesitating before they shift lower.

I'm naked. I shucked that towel before I crawled into bed, and now I'm thanking the good lord above because those fingers are on my dick, and they're stroking.

Squeezing.

I pop my eyes open and stare at the ceiling for a moment, reveling in the touch. A thumb swirls around the top of my cock, again and again and then her mouth…

Fuck.

"Fuck," I bite out, glancing down to find Maisey sprawled between my legs, her thick hair everywhere, lush pink lips wrapped tight around my dick. She looks up, her eyes flashing when they catch mine, and she releases her hold on me with a loud pop.

"You're awake."

"So are you," I say through clenched teeth.

"I couldn't resist." She has my erection in her grip, and she slides her fingers up, then down, nice and firm. "I hope you don't think I was trying to take advantage of you. I could tell you were waking up."

"This beats my alarm, that's for damn sure," I say, making her laugh.

I could wake up like this every day for the rest of my life, and I wouldn't protest.

Her laughter dies the longer we maintain eye contact and then she slips my cock back into her mouth, her eyes sliding shut, a low moan sounding in her throat. I watch in fascination as she works me into a near frenzy, her fingers curled tight around the base of my dick, her lips sucking, her tongue licking.

Jesus.

I am done for.

"Not like this," I finally say minutes later, reaching for her, pulling her up with ease, flipping her around so she's lying flat on her back, and I'm right above her. "Let me look at you first."

She removed the robe sometime during the night. And I know it's definitely night. The room is dark, even with the curtains cracked open, and I can barely make out her features.

I need to remedy that problem quick.

Reaching over, I flick on the bedside lamp and she closes her eyes against the harsh light that bathes the room.

"You should turn it off," she protests as she slings her arm over her eyes.

Putting her breasts on perfect display.

"And miss seeing you naked and in my bed?" I actually snort. "Hell to the no."

Maisey laughs again, making her breasts jiggle, and I watch, my mouth going dry. Her laughter slowly dies and then she's reaching for me.

And I'm going to her.

Kissing her like I might die at any moment and this is my last chance to taste her.

Racing my lips down the elegant length of her neck.

Breathing her in.

Cupping her breasts, circling her pink nipples.

With my tongue.

Drawing them into my mouth.

I feast on her chest, slip my hand along her curving belly until I'm touching her between her legs. She spreads them, the sheets shift, and her sigh escapes when I make contact with her hot, wet flesh.

God, she tastes good. Feels even better. I press the spot I know she likes best—funny how we don't forget that—and she lifts her hips, moaning my name.

My cock is throbbing. My entire body is throbbing. I remember I have a condom in my wallet—one lone condom in my wallet, that's fucking it—and I press my face into the mattress with a groan.

"What's wrong?" she asks, pushing at my shoulder.

I lift my head to study her. She's so fucking beautiful. And I only get one chance to actually be inside her tonight, so I better make it good. "I only brought one condom."

She smiles. Shakes her head. "Then we better put it to good use."

Chapter Thirteen

Maisey

I thought he was going to tell me something terrible, the way he moaned in agony like the world was coming to end.

Only one condom? No big deal.

There are *so* many other things we can do tonight.

He resumes his position, hovering above me, all of his attention focused on my body, which feels like it's been set on fire. Such intense concentration zeroed in on me, it's almost too much.

Almost.

With his mouth on my belly, those big, capable hands are on the inside of my thighs as they push me wide open. Everything inside of me is drawn tight in anticipation of what he's going to do next. My body remembers how good he was at it.

And the moment his lips touch me there, in my most sensitive, secretive space, I know he's still just as good.

Perhaps even better.

He licks and sucks and searches and breathes. Yes, just his breath on my flesh sends a shudder through me, makes me clench my eyes shut tight, my fingers buried in his hair, holding him to me like he plans on escaping.

No way. Uh uh. He's not going anywhere.

His fingers push inside me. One. Two. Three. His lips lock around my clit, sucking, licking, sucking again. I'm losing all control, thrashing beneath him, reaching, reaching, reaching for that spot. That bright, white spot that's going to wash over me, pull me under, make me see stars...

Oh. Right there. Yes, right there. I say it out loud, trying to keep him in place, and he doesn't move. Just keeps doing the same thing, again and again, because he knows I'm close. I'm so close. Chanting his name over and over again until I'm coming. I fall right over that delicious edge, let his lips and his tongue and his fingers pull me under, seeing nothing but blinding white stars.

I'm a melted heap of flesh and bone after he's finished with me, and when he slides up to lie by my side, I crack open my eyes to find a very satisfied smile curling his perfect lips.

"You liked that," he says, and it's not a question.

"I'm not going to answer you," I say primly, closing my eyes and breathing deep. I'm trying to calm my still racing heart but it's difficult. Especially with him next to me, his fully erect cock brushing against my thigh.

"You fucking loved it," he whispers close to my ear, just before he nibbles it. His hand is on my waist as he rolls me toward him and I press my body against his, trapping his cock between us.

I am desperate to have him inside me.

"You're right." I grab hold of him and pull, so that we roll until he's on top of me. He's heavy, his weight pressing me into the mattress, and it feels so good. He's such a big, muscular man, and I love it.

I absolutely love it.

"Maybe we should wait a—" he starts but I cut him off with a kiss, my tongue seeking his. Minutes later he comes up for air and mutters, "Okay, we definitely shouldn't wait."

And then he's gone, crawling out of bed, going in search of his wallet, which I know he finds in less than a minute, if his triumphant "Ah-ha" is any indication.

He crawls back into bed, his weight making the mattress dip, and then he's there, condom in hand, gathering me into his arms and holding me close.

"I've dreamed of this moment since I was fifteen years old," he admits, his voice, his gaze so very, very serious.

"Really?" I reach up, brushing his hair away from his forehead. "Fifteen?"

"That's when we got together. My sophomore year and your

freshman year," he reminds me.

I'm still brushing his hair, sifting the soft strands through my fingers. "We were so young."

"I thought you were the hottest thing alive."

I tilt my head, contemplating him. "Seriously?"

Nodding, he reaches out, tapping the tip of my nose with his index finger. "Really."

"I didn't understand why an older boy was interested in me," I confess.

"You were so cute and funny."

"I was a big nerd," I remind him.

"Not true." He replaces his finger with his lips, kissing my nose. "You were beautiful. You still are. And you were so damn smart. You made me laugh. You made me do things I never would've done."

"Like go to a craft fair." That was one of our first dates. My mom dropping us off at the local craft fair so we could walk around and look at the booths and eat food, holding hands the entire time.

It was the dreamiest first date ever.

"I only did it to be with you." He kisses me, his lips extra soft. "I can't believe we're here. Right now. All these years later."

What do you mean?

I want to ask him that question, but I'm scared to know the answer. Maybe what we're doing means nothing to him. In his eyes, this could be all fun. Nothing serious. A chance to consummate the relationship we started all those years ago.

He could leave, and I'd never see him again.

The lump that forms in my throat at the thought is hard to swallow past.

We start kissing again. Long, tongue-filled kisses, our hands wandering, searching. My body is languid, my senses on overload as he caresses me everywhere and by the time his fingers land between my legs, I am a panting, desperate ball of need.

He tears at the condom wrapper with ease and I watch as he rolls it on, sheathing himself completely. I swallow hard, wondering what it will feel like to have that much length inside of me, and then the thought leaves my brain the moment he positions himself above me, his erection probing at the juncture between my legs, his hands braced on either side of my head.

His mouth finds mine. Again. His hands find mine, linking our fingers together and bringing my arms up so they're above my head. His gaze finds mine, holds it as he oh so slowly enters me, one delicious inch at a time.

I close my eyes. Arch against him as he sinks deep. Deeper. He groans and the sound ripples through me as I wait for him to begin to move.

"Maisey," he whispers. "Open your eyes."

I do as he says to find him watching me, his gaze full of so much tender emotion my heart feels like it just cracked wide open, spilling its contents everywhere. I press my lips together, struggling to keep my composure and I can tell he knows.

He knows.

Without hesitation he kisses me, a chaste, sweet kiss as he starts to move. I remove my hands from his so I can run them up and down his back as he slides deep inside, pulls almost all the way out, only to plunge deep once again. This feels so good. *He* feels so good. I don't ever want it—or him—to stop.

We move, slow and languid at first, learning each other's pace. I'm in no hurry, I've already had my release, but I can feel the tension in the line of Tucker's shoulders, see the tightness of his jaw, how his lips have gone thin.

"Let go," I whisper, placing my hand on his cheek, caressing his stubble-covered skin. His gaze meets mine, hungry and frantic, and I smile up at him. "Please. Don't hold back on my account, Tucker."

It's like my words grant him permission. He grabs hold of my hip, repositioning me just so, and then he's pounding deep inside me, going hard, our skin slapping, his grunts growing louder. He's unleashing everything he has on me, until I'm helpless. Swept up into the storm that is Tucker McCloud.

Never before has a man been so—*primal* toward me. He doesn't handle me like I'm made of porcelain. More like he's extra rough, and the best thing about this?

He knows I can take it.

And I can. Oh God, I can totally take it, and having him like this is…incredible. This moment is incredible. So perfect. So right. And just like that my orgasm is looming. Hovering just beyond where I can reach it, and Tucker's every thrust draws it closer. Closer…

"Oh fuck, Maise," he whispers, his voice harsh, his panting breath stirring the hair at my temple. I run my hands down his smooth back, settle my palms against his ass, and push him closer.

As close as I can get him.

He comes with a shout, his big body shuddering as he presses his sweaty forehead to mine while taking big, gulping breaths. I cup the back of his head, keeping him close, my own orgasm sweeping over me, sweet and quick and stinging sharp. So sharp it brings tears to my eyes.

Something snaps deep inside me, breaking apart, flooding my senses. I close my eyes, fighting against it, praying I don't fall apart in front of Tucker.

I know this feeling I'm experiencing. I'm familiar with it, though it's been a while.

It's good old fashioned love.

Chapter Fourteen

Tucker

So far, I've lead an interesting life. I've done a lot of things. I've accomplished goals that most people only dream of. I've traveled the world, I've met lots of people, and I've worked in a variety of cities.

But this past week? Hands down, it's been one of the best of my life.

Like, no joke. The weirdest thing that's bringing me joy? All the planning—working out the details for my parents' anniversary party with my sisters. If we're not texting, we're talking on the phone, and if we're not talking on the phone, we're actually together, and I've actually had…

A great time.

The party has brought Stella, Georgia, and me closer, and if I'm being honest with myself, I've never been very close with my sisters. Until this week. We've gone to a party supply store together, we showed each other our costumes, we ordered flowers from Maisey's sister Brooke, and we helped Maisey come up with the final design for the cake.

When I was a teenager, I remember feeling like I had to get out of here as soon as possible. The small-town vibe stifled me. I felt like I was going nowhere, and I knew, I just freaking *knew,* that I could be someone…

Somewhere else. Anywhere else.

Being back home after being gone for so long has made me

appreciate Cunningham Falls. Made me appreciate the townspeople who remember me. I've missed out on a lot with my family, with my old friends.

This week has been a lot of fun. If I'm being completely honest with myself, I don't want it to end.

And then of course, there's Maisey. She's the main reason I've had such a great week. Spending so much time with her just doing…regular things. Hanging out, going to dinner, enjoying her actually making me dinner, watching movies on Netflix or going to the movies, having her over to my sister's house so we can go over the final details for the anniversary party…

We've spent so much time together, it's like we're a real couple.

Last weekend, I helped Maisey deliver a wedding cake to a bridal client. Talk about an experience. It was a trip, watching her work her chaotic magic, hustling those cakes into the reception hall at one wedding, and the very hotel I'm staying at for another. Once she'd delivered the cake and we were on our way back to her place, I couldn't help but lean over and give her a smacking kiss on the cheek while she drove.

"What was that for?" she'd asked, smiling at me as I settled back into my seat.

"You're amazing," I told her, because she was.

Is.

By the way, I'm in love with her.

This isn't a new realization. I've known this from the moment I ran into her my first weekend back home. Seeing her rattled me, but in the best possible way. From that night on, I wanted her. I've always wanted her.

But not just sexually. I crave her company. Her sweetness. Her silly jokes. Her laugh.

God, her laugh.

How can we make this work? I want to make it work. I want her to be mine in every possible way, yet she lives here and I live in California. I'm at the height of my career, finally finding my place with a team, relieved that they have no desire to trade me. I'm happy in San Francisco, with my Niners.

Maisey? She's happy here too. She has her own business, she's doing well. How can I expect her to close her business and move to a new state, change her entire life, just for me?

I can't.

For once in my life, I don't know what to do.

"Oh my God, this cake is a complete pain in my ass."

I chuckle under my breath when I hear Maisey complain from the kitchen. She's working on my parents' cake at home, though first she baked it in the industrial-sized oven at Cake Nation, then brought the cakes home when they cooled so she can frost them here. She claims she can concentrate better when she's at her place, but I don't believe her.

I think she just wanted to hang out with me.

"Why is the cake such a pain in your ass?" I ask her as I walk into the kitchen a minute later.

She glances up at me, blowing the wayward hair out of her eyes with a frustrated breath, a frosting tube clutched in her hands. "Soooo many lines on this, and they have to be perfect," she says, drawing the words out. "I can't screw up. There's no room for me to make a mistake."

"You've got this." I come up behind her, settling my hands on her shoulders. She's so tight, I immediately start massaging them, easing the knots from her muscles with the hard press of my fingers. "So tense."

"Hunching over a cake for hours on end isn't good for you," she says, sucking her lower lip between her teeth as she draws a gold line of frosting on the cake.

"I know something that'll make you feel better," I whisper close to her ear.

She smiles, but shakes her head. "I have to finish this tier first."

Damn. Guess I'll have to wait. The sex between us has been unbelievable. I can't get enough of her. And I don't think she can get enough of me either. We've done it *everywhere*.

Everywhere.

When I'm done massaging her shoulders, I move so I'm sitting at the table across from her, watching her work. "Found out today a few of my friends are coming to my parents' party."

"Friends from school?" she asks, her gaze still locked on the cake as she draws line after line of frosting.

"No, friends from my team. Football players."

She glances up at me. "Who?"

"Jordan Tuttle and Cannon Whittaker. They go way back, went to high school together. They've been good to me since I've joined the team," I explain. "And they were both so nice to my parents when they came to visit last season, I had to put the offer out there. Didn't expect them to accept, but they'll be here this weekend."

"How cool." She doesn't sound that interested, but I think it's because she's so overwhelmed with decorating the cake.

Yet I still can't help but feel a little butt hurt.

"They fly in tomorrow." I stare at her for a moment, waiting for her to look at me, but she doesn't take her focus away from the cake. Is it rational to be jealous of food? Probably not. "I'm hoping we can all go to dinner together tomorrow night. Tuttle brought his fiancée and so did Cannon."

"They're both engaged?"

"Yeah, they are." I'm a little envious of their relationships too. They both fell head over heels in love with their women, though Jordan never really fell out of love with Amanda since they were high school sweethearts.

I can totally relate.

"I'd love to meet them. As long as this cake will be done in time. Oh, and I have to finish the wedding cakes for this weekend." She's gnawing on her lower lip again, her laser focus concentration in full effect.

"You can do it," I say with all the confidence of someone who doesn't have to work on anything. "I have faith in you."

"Gee, thanks." Her voice is sarcastic. "Glad to know you're by my side."

I rear back in my chair, confused. She's acting pissed. It's gotta be stress. I've given her no reason to be stressed out or upset. I've been the perfect boyfriend this last week.

The perfect *temporary* boyfriend.

Shit. Maybe that's the problem.

"If you don't want to go to dinner tomorrow, it's cool," I say, keeping my voice even. I don't want to show I'm angry. I'm not really angry.

But if I keep poking at her, provoking her, then I'm going to cause a fight.

Sighing, she sets the frosting tube down, pushing her hair away from her forehead before she blows an exasperated breath. "I'm sorry if I'm being a jerk. I definitely want to go, but I won't be able to if this cake isn't finished. Plus, I have the wedding cakes to do. Thank God, they're not too outrageous." She props her elbow on the table, rubbing at her temple as she remains quiet. Unease slips through me and I wait for her to say something else.

With a heavy sigh she says, "I have to be honest with you, Tucker. I'm claiming I'll get it all done, but I won't. I know I won't. I have too much to do, I'm feeling overwhelmed, and there's no way I can make time for dinner with your friends tomorrow. I'm so sorry."

I sit there, blinking at her. I should appreciate her honesty. I *do* appreciate it. But I also feel like she's not making enough time for me, and it…sucks.

I make time for her. All I want is to devote myself to her completely.

Clearly she doesn't feel the same way.

"You're busy. I get it." I'm busy from August until February—if we make the playoffs and ultimately, the Super Bowl. That hasn't happened in my career yet, but I know busy. I've experienced it enough that sometimes I forgot where I was, especially in the early years of my career.

She's studying me, her gaze narrowed.

Uh oh.

"You don't have to act so pouty," she says.

"I'm not pouting," I immediately return.

At least, I didn't think I was.

"This is my life." She waves her hands around the dining room area, her expression irritable. "This is what I do. And I know I'm overextended. I do too much, I don't know how to say no, and you know what? I'm okay with that. I want to be busy. I *need* this. I need to grow my career, and make Cake Nation a total success. Don't get me wrong, I'm happy now, but I want more. I *deserve* more."

"I agree. You do deserve more. You work damn hard, and I'm so proud of you. You can do so much—" I start to say, but she cuts me off.

"Right. I know. This is the only thing I've done on my own, and I can't throw it away for someone else. For something that has no guarantees." Her chest is rising and falling frantically, her lips parted, her eyes wide, and I'm…

Confused by her reaction.

"What exactly are you saying, Maise?"

"I don't know! The real question is, what exactly are we *doing?* We act like we're together. I always want to spend time with you. I think you feel the same way. But can't you see that what we're doing is impossible?" She shakes her head when I start to talk and I remain quiet. Note the unshed tears in her eyes, making them shine. "I watched my sister and her husband suffer through this. Though their circumstance is different, and Brody was able to move his business here. I don't have that option, and neither do you."

Actually, she does have that option. I'm guessing she just doesn't want to.

"Long distance relationships can work," I suggest and she's shaking her head repeatedly.

She doesn't want to hear it.

"We can't play at a real couple anymore, Tucker. No matter how badly I want to. In the end, I'm going to get hurt again, and I can't risk it." A single tear falls, sliding a damp path down her cheek and I'm tempted to reach across the table and catch it with my thumb.

I hate to see her cry.

"I would never hurt you." I rise to my feet, glaring at her, hating the flash of hurt, the flash of pain that streaks through me, sticking low in my gut. She's basically kicking me out. Why? Because she cares about me too much? "That is the last thing I want to do."

"Too late." Her smile is tremulous, like she's about to break at any moment. "You already did."

Chapter Fifteen

Maisey

How I made it through the last few days, I'm not sure. After Tucker left my house that night, I broke down. Forget frosting his parents' cake. All I could do was cry.

And cry and cry and cry.

Maybe I got it all out of my system, because the next day, it was business as usual. Or maybe it was because that's all I could manage—cry for a few hours, then get back on my feet. I had things to do. A business to run.

I keep telling myself it was for the best, me ending it with Tucker right then and there. I have to protect myself, and him too. While it's been a lot of fun, spending time with Tucker, and I know if circumstances were different, we could totally make it work. But I refuse to offer up my heart to him one more time, only for him to crush it.

No way could I suffer through that again.

So I concentrated on my work. The wedding cakes both turned out fabulous. Once they were done, I returned to the project I started, and I finished the McCloud anniversary cake late Saturday night.

And now it's Sunday evening. I delivered and set up the cake a few hours ago, then rushed home, took a shower, and curled my hair into a 1920s style accompanied by a sequined headband and a feather. I carefully applied my makeup, told myself I would not cry tonight, and I arrived at the party fashionably late, wearing my gorgeous black and gold sequined flapper dress.

No way was I going to waste the forty-five bucks I spent on this dress I ordered from Amazon Prime. It's beautiful. Form fitting, sleeveless, the hem made out of long black fringe, this costume makes me feel like a movie star. Wearing it is making me act more confident than I feel, which is a good thing.

I'm going to need as much confidence as I can muster tonight.

As I enter the ballroom where the party is being held, I see plenty of friends, including most of the McCloud family, and they all wave at me with giant grins on their faces. Seeing everyone renews my feeling that coming tonight was the right choice. I don't have to skip out on this celebration to save Tucker's feelings.

Besides, let him catch one last glimpse of me in this dress, just before I strut out of his life for good.

The party is in full swing. Servers move about the room carrying trays laden with appetizers or flutes of champagne. The place is decorated in black and gold streamers, and there are giant number-shaped balloons everywhere—so many 40s I wonder how many they bought. There's a DJ on a platform right in front of the makeshift dance floor, and the music—currently a song from The Great Gatsby soundtrack—is loud. I see Tucker's parents out on the dance floor kicking it up, both of them laughing.

My heart kicks as I stop to watch them. To have such a strong love like theirs, to be there for each other unconditionally for the last forty years…

What would that be like? I can't imagine it. Don't think I'll ever be lucky enough to experience something like that either.

"You showed up."

I turn to find Stella McCloud standing in front of me, gorgeous in a black sequin and lace dress that faintly resembles mine, clutching a glass of champagne.

"I did," I tell her. From the way she's looking at me, I hope she's not mad. "I was invited."

"Right. I know you were." Stella smiles, but it doesn't quite reach her eyes. "But you broke my brother's heart."

Her simple words gut me, but I champion through it. Fake it till you make it, right? "He'll be fine. Seriously. He'll go back to California and forget all about me."

"I don't think so." Stella shakes her head and takes a step closer, her voice lowering. "He came over to my house last night, and we talked for a while. I swear he was going to cry."

Oh my God. "Why would he cry?" I've never seen Tucker cry.

Ever.

"He misses you. Like I said, you broke his heart, Maisey. And plus, he was hanging out with his friends and their girlfriends and he said it made him realize he's never going to find someone who's perfect for him. Well. He did say he found her." She sends me a pointed look. "But she doesn't feel the same."

I feel the same way, I want to scream at her.

"It won't work," I tell her, grabbing hold of her hands and squeezing hard as I stare into her eyes. I'm trying to convince her that I'm right. I'm also trying to convince myself. "I want it to, but it won't. It didn't before."

"That's because you two were young and he stupidly broke up with you," Stella reminds me.

"The circumstances haven't necessarily changed. He lives and works in another state. I live and work here. My life is here," I say as I release Stella's hands.

She pulls me into a quick hug and asks quietly, "But where's your heart?"

My entire body prickles with awareness and I know someone is watching us. Watching me. I know who that someone is too.

Glancing over my shoulder, I spot Tucker across the room, flanked on either side by men who are just as tall, broad, and handsome as he is. He's wearing a black suit, and he looks incredibly gorgeous. So gorgeous, just staring at him is making my entire body ache.

His intense gaze is locked on me. His expression like stone, his eyes...

Like fire.

That fire, passion, emotion, is all for me.

I turn away, my gaze meeting Stella's once more, who's watching me with a knowing look. I'm sure she just witnessed that little moment, and I need to act like it meant nothing. "He'll be better off without me."

"Yeah. Keep telling yourself that," Stella says with a sigh and a shake of her head, just before she walks away.

Leaving me all alone.

I grab a glass of champagne from a passing server and down all of it in one swallow, setting the empty glass on a nearby table. I'm standing on the sidelines of the dance floor, watching everyone laugh and shout and have a good time. Brooke and Brody are dancing, and the smile on my sister's face is one of pure, unadulterated joy. I've never seen her look happier. It's all because she found her true love, fought for it, waited for it, and he came back to her.

They are meant to be.

Me? I'm miserable. Thinking about what I said to Stella. What she said to me. My life is here, but my heart is with Tucker.

And when he leaves, he'll take my heart with him.

Chapter Sixteen

Tucker

"That's her, huh?" my friend and 49er quarterback Jordan Tuttle asks me, indicating Maisey with a casual nod in her direction. She's across the room, my sister has just walked away from her, and I can't stop staring. I want to go to her. I'm desperate to go to her.

But I can't. She told me how she felt. She doesn't want to continue this.

She doesn't want me.

"That's her," I murmur, bringing my champagne glass to my lips, but I don't drink. Instead, I'm staring at the golden, bubbly alcohol, fizzing like it's a living, breathing thing. You drink champagne to celebrate something, and though yes, my parents have something pretty major to celebrate, I don't.

I'm not feeling this party, the joyous mood, none of it. I can't even make myself drink champagne. It all feels like a lie.

Everyone's having the time of their lives, and I'm a miserable, sad sack of shit.

"She's beautiful," Jordan says, nudging me with his elbow, making me wince. "You should go talk to her."

"Hell, no." I take a sip of the champagne, make a face, and set it on the empty tray of a passing server.

"Why not?" This from Cannon's fiancée, Lady Susanna Sumner. That's a mouthful, am I right? She's nobility, her dad is an earl or whatever—I have no idea what that means—but it feels like Cannon is marrying into the royal family. He's become a huge celebrity in the U.K. these last few months, which is crazy.

"She dumped me a few days ago," I say, my voice tight.

Susanna frowns. She has the biggest blue eyes I've ever seen and they're blinking up at me at this very moment. "Look at her right now. She seems so sad—as sad as you. I'm sure she didn't mean it."

"Oh, she meant every word she said," I say with a chuckle that doesn't hold even a hint of humor.

"Sometimes we say things we regret." Susanna rests her small hand on my forearm. "Haven't you ever said anything you regret?"

All the time. I have numerous regrets, most of them having to do with Maisey.

"I think Susanna's right," Jordan says, and she turns to gape at him, which makes me think this doesn't happen often. "You should go talk to her."

"And what do I say to her?" I ask him.

Cannon chooses that moment to appear by his future wife's side, slinging his arm over her shoulders. He's been the hit of the night, dancing with all of my mom's friends, joking with the guys, taking photos with everyone, and having the time of his life. For being such a large, quiet man, he definitely knows when to turn it on and socialize. "Tell her how you really feel," he says to me just before he drops a kiss on top of Susanna's blonde head.

"How do you even know what we're talking about?" I ask him irritably.

"It's all you've been talking about since we got here," Cannon answers, shaking his head. Like he's disappointed in me. "Man up and let her know that you're willing to do anything to make this work."

How can I admit putting myself out there—one more time—is terrifying? I sound like a wimp. "What if she rejects me again?" I ask. That's my biggest fear. She rejected me once already a few days ago. She's most likely going to do it again.

Is this some sort of revenge thing because of what I did to her when we were teenagers? God, I hope not.

"She won't," Jordan says quietly, with all the assurance of someone who's got the love of his life by his side and has zero fears.

I don't know what to do.

"If she does reject you, then at least you tried." Susanna smiles up at me. "And you can't regret that. You have to at least try, right?"

She's right. They're all right. But when can I talk to her? Now? In the middle of my parents' party? They haven't even cut the cake yet.

"I'll be back," I tell my friends just before I leave them to walk across the room.

"Go get her!" Susanna yells after me, making me crack a smile.

The first real smile I've had in days.

I search the crowded room, but I can't find her. And so many of the women are wearing similar dresses, it's hard to discern who's who. I find her sister, but Brooke tells me she hasn't really talked to Maisey since she arrived.

It's like she's disappeared.

I head for the outside patio and that's where I find her. Hiding in the farthest corner, away from everyone, sitting on the rock ledge, the 1920s flapper clutching her iPhone—such a contradiction.

A beautiful one.

My heart cracks at seeing her, and I'm afraid it won't close back up until she agrees that we can make this work.

With determined steps, I make my way over to Maisey.

The girl I'm in love with.

The girl I can't let go.

"Hey," I say quietly when I'm standing in front of her.

She glances up from her phone, blinking in seeming shock when she realizes it's me. "Hey."

"You look beautiful." The words trip out of me, like I can't contain them. But it's true. She's gorgeous in her dress, her hair, her dark eyes and ruby red lips.

I want to kiss all that lipstick off her mouth.

"Thank you." Her cheeks are the faintest pink and her gaze rushes over me. "You look handsome."

I'd planned on taking photos of the two of us together. Maybe even taking a few photos with my parents, my family.

What a dumb sap I am.

"Thanks." I run a nervous hand through my hair, glancing around to make sure no one is nearby before I say, "Can I talk to you for a minute?"

Dare I think her expression turns hopeful? "Sure," she says, nodding toward the empty spot beside her. "Sit down."

I do as she says, sitting way closer to her than I need to. So close our thighs press against each other, and I can smell her delectable scent. "Are you having fun?" I ask.

"No," she says with a sad smile. God, she's killing me. "Not really."

"Then why did you come?" I want to touch her. Reach out and grab her hand. Caress her cheek. Touch her hair. Something. *Anything.*

She makes me yearn. Fuck, she makes me desperate.

"I don't know." She shrugs, looking away from me. "I thought I was doing the right thing, coming to this party and celebrating your parents. Spend some time with my friends, dress up in a fun costume and drink lots of alcohol. But I'm here, and it's like I don't want to talk to anyone. No one really wants to talk to me either. I guess I'd rather be alone in my misery."

"Would you rather not talk to me?" I will get up and walk away from her right now if that's what she wants. I don't mean to upset her, but I have to give this—*us*—at least one more try.

I just…I have to.

"No, I want to talk to you. I do. It's just…" She shrugs again. "I'm sure you're mad at me. Why would you want to talk to me?"

I give in to my urges and grab her hand. Her fingers are trembling and I interlock them with mine, squeezing her hand tight. "I'm not mad at you."

Maisey gazes up at me, her brown eyes full of so much sadness. "You're not?"

I shake my head, trying to find the right words to say to her. I don't want to screw this up. "I could never be mad at you. Not for long, at least."

The barest smile curves her lips, but she doesn't say anything.

"Maise." I take a deep breath, hating the nerves that suddenly fill me. I can do this. I can tell her how much she means to me. "I know you said you wanted to end this—us, but I'm not ready to let you go yet."

Now she's frowning at me. But she's still not talking.

"You mean too much to me. You always have." I squeeze her hand again and try to smile, but it proves difficult. I'm too damn nervous. "I'm in love with you, Maisey."

Her mouth drops open and she pulls her hand out of my grip.

"I am," I tell her before she can say anything else. Tell me I'm crazy or whatever. "I don't think I ever got over you. I *know* I never got over you. Not when I was eighteen and like an idiot I broke up with you. Not after all these years, when I didn't know what you were doing, or where you were, yet you were here all this time, almost like you were...waiting for me."

"I was definitely not waiting for you," she retorts, sounding irritated.

Her protest feels so familiar I want to laugh. Typical Maisey.

"Fine, you weren't waiting for me." I bump her shoulder with mine. "Listen, I told myself I couldn't commit to anyone because I was too busy. I moved too much, I worked too much. How could I ever have time for someone? Have time for a serious relationship?"

"Then...how can you find time for a relationship now?" she asks, her voice faint.

"I didn't have time then because I didn't want to make time. No one I met over the years could ever compare to you, Maise." I reach out with my free hand and brush a strand of hair away from her cheek. "You're it for me. You're the only one I want. The only one I need."

She remains quiet for a while and the silence nearly kills me. Tears my nerves to shreds. I'm bouncing my knee, my heart is racing, and I feel like I'm going to explode from the waiting. The anticipation.

The fear that she's going to tell me to fuck off once and for all.

Chapter Seventeen

Maisey

Tucker just said that he's in love with me. That I'm it for him. I'm the only one he needs.

My heart feels like it's going to burst with happiness. Though I still have a few concerns…

"You live in San Francisco, Tucker," I say, my voice quiet, my thoughts in utter chaos. "And I live here. In Montana. I don't know how we're ever going to see each other."

"We can make it work." He scoots even closer to me, and his hard, muscular thigh burns through my sequined skirt. "If we want it bad enough, we can make anything work."

I want to believe him so badly. "What about all those crazy women who throw themselves at you?" When he gives me a confused look, I continue, "Your fans. I know you have them. You're gorgeous. You're famous. I'm sure you have crazed fan girls everywhere."

He is full blown grinning. "Don't worry, none of them notice me. They all love Tuttle more."

"Whatever." I roll my eyes, leaning into him. "I won't be able to go to all your games."

"You can come to any game you want." He grabs my hand once more and lifts it to his mouth, dropping a kiss on my knuckles. "And I'm busy only about seven months out of the year. The other five months, I can be here most of the time."

"Really?" That doesn't sound so bad.

Oh my God, am I crazy for thinking this could work?

"Really," he says, his voice firm, his gaze…intense.

This man. This beautiful, wonderful, funny, sweet man, is in love with me. He's always been in love with me. This is the second chance that I never thought I'd get, and I should…

I should.

Take it.

"I'm in love with you too," I murmur, and his eyes widen the moment the words pass my lips.

"Wait a minute. What did you just say? Repeat that again." He cups his free hand around his ear and leans in closer.

"Stop." I shove his shoulder, but it's like trying to push a brick wall. He is so freaking built. "You heard me."

His smile fades and his expression turns sincere, his voice softening when he confesses, "I really need to hear you say it again, Maise."

Never taking my eyes from his, I repeat, "I'm in love with you, Tucker."

His smile is so wide I'm afraid he's going to strain a face muscle. "I love you too."

"And I want to try and make this work. I do." I take a deep breath, a faint laugh escaping me. "It'll probably be a little crazy for a while, and I might get mad at you sometimes. And you'll probably get mad at me too, but I love you too much to let you go."

He lets go of my hand and cups my face with his palms, his thumbs caressing my cheeks. "You really mean it, don't you?"

I nod, my smile trembling, my eyes filling with tears. "I mean it."

His mouth lands on mine, stealing any other words I might've said. Stealing my breath. Stealing my heart.

There's nothing else for me to say anyway.

Chapter Eighteen

Maisey

Six months later

Have you heard from him yet?

Chewing on my lower lip, I study the text from my sister, wishing I could give her a different answer.

Nope.

She immediately texts back.

You think he's all right? It's snowing really hard right now.

Ugh. I could punch my sister for trying to make me worry more than I already am.

Thanks for being so positive!

My reply is full of sarcasm. Hopefully she realizes that.

I'm sorry! I'm worried about him, she replies.

So am I. I'll let you know when he gets home, I type, then toss my phone aside.

Home. The man of my dreams is on his way home, to our new house we share in Cunningham Falls, driving in an almost-blizzard to get here for Christmas.

I can't wait to see him, and after I hug him, I might sock him in the stomach for making me worry so bad.

I told him he could take his time. It's only the twenty-third. We still have another twenty-four hours before Christmas is here, but he said no way. He had to get here tonight.

And so I wait. It's soon past ten o'clock, the roads are probably a nightmare, the snow is starting to fall even harder, and I want to cry.

But then light flashes in the window facing the street and I hear a car engine pulling into our driveway. Relief floods me, making me weak, and I rise from the couch, practically running to the door in the kitchen that leads out to the garage.

The door swings open minutes later and I rush forward, tackle hugging him as tight as I can.

"Well, hello to you too," he says, amusement lacing his voice as he wraps me up in his thick arms.

"I was worried sick." My voice is muffled against his chest, and I burrow my face closer. He smells so good. I've missed him. I always miss him. Having him come home after being away is the best thing ever.

His leaving is also the worst thing ever.

But we're making it work. Because we love each other.

"I know. Sorry. I probably shouldn't have driven home tonight, but I had to. I wanted to see you." He grabs hold of my arms and steps away so he can take me in. He whistles low, shaking his head. "You are a sight for sore eyes."

"I missed you," I admit just before he sweeps me back into his arms and thoroughly kisses me.

God, I love his thorough kisses.

"Come on, let's go sit by the tree." He hooks his arm around my shoulders and guides me back into the living room, falling onto the couch and dragging me with him. I rest my head on his chest as we both stare at the decorated Christmas tree sitting in front of the window, the multi-colored lights twinkling.

He reaches over and turns off the lamp, the tree the only thing glowing in the room, and the sigh that escapes him is full of contentment.

"I could sit like this with you forever," he admits, his mouth right at my temple before he kisses me there.

"That sounds dreamy," I agree in a faint whisper.

"What do you want for Christmas?" he asks me minutes later, startling me. I thought he'd fallen asleep. I was almost asleep myself, lulled by the sound of his steady heartbeat.

"I already have everything I could ever want." I tilt my head back, smiling up at him. "I don't need anything else."

"Not even a trip to Maui?" he asks, eyebrows raised. "In February? For Valentine's Day? What do you think?"

"That's a lot of questions to ask me right now," I tease and he rolls his eyes. "I think that sounds amazing."

"I think you're amazing." He kisses me again, his lips lingering. "I love you, Maise."

"I love you too, Tucker."

And I do.

Sign up for the 1001 Dark Nights Newsletter
and be entered to win a Tiffany Lock necklace.

There's a contest every quarter!

Go to www.1001DarkNights.com to subscribe.

As a bonus, all subscribers can download
FIVE FREE exclusive books!

Discover the Kristen Proby Crossover Collection

Soaring with Fallon: A Big Sky Novel
By Kristen Proby

Fallon McCarthy has climbed the corporate ladder. She's had the office with the view, the staff, and the plaque on her door. The unexpected loss of her grandmother taught her that there's more to life than meetings and conference calls, so she quit, and is happy to be a nomad, checking off items on her bucket list as she takes jobs teaching yoga in each place she lands in. She's happy being free, and has no interest in being tied down.

When Noah King gets the call that an eagle has been injured, he's not expecting to find a beautiful stranger standing vigil when he arrives. Rehabilitating birds of prey is Noah's passion, it's what he lives for, and he doesn't have time for a nosy woman who's suddenly taken an interest in Spread Your Wings sanctuary.

But Fallon's gentle nature, and the way she makes him laugh, and *feel* again draws him in. When it comes time for Fallon to move on, will Noah's love be enough for her to stay, or will he have to find the strength to let her fly?

* * * *

Wicked Force: A Wicked Horse Vegas/Big Sky Novella
By Sawyer Bennett

From *New York Times* and *USA Today* bestselling author Sawyer Bennett...

Joslyn Meyers has taken the celebrity world by storm, drawing the attention of millions. But one fan's affections has gone too far, and she's running to the one place she hopes he'll never find her – back home to Cunningham Falls.

Kynan McGrath leads The Jameson Group, a world-class security organization, and he's ready to do what it takes to keep Joslyn safe, even if it means giving up his own life in return. The one thing he's not prepared to lose, though, is his heart.

* * * *

Crazy Imperfect Love: A Dirty Dicks/Big Sky Novella
By KL Grayson

From *USA Today* bestselling author KL Grayson…

Abigail Darwin needs one thing in life: consistency. Okay, make that two things: consistency and order. Tired of being shackled to her obsessive-compulsive mind, Abigail is determined to break free. Which is why she's shaking things up.

Fresh out of nursing school, she takes a traveling nurse position. A new job in a new city every few months? That's a sure-fire way to keep her from settling down and falling into old habits. First stop, Cunningham Falls, Montana.

The only problem? She didn't plan on falling in love with the quaint little town, and she sure as heck didn't plan on falling for its resident surgeon, Dr. Drake Merritt

Laid back, messy, and spontaneous, Drake is everything she's not. But he is completely smitten by the new, quirky nurse working on the med-surg floor of the hospital.

Abby puts up a good fight, but Drake is determined to break through her carefully erected walls to find out what makes her tick. And sigh and moan and smile and laugh. Because he really loves her laugh.

But falling in love isn't part of Abby's plan. Will Drake have what it takes to convince her that the best things in life come from doing what scares us the most?

* * * *

Worth Fighting For: A Warrior Fight Club/Big Sky Novella
By Laura Kaye

From *New York Times* and *USA Today* bestselling author Laura Kaye...

Getting in deep has never felt this good...

Commercial diving instructor Tara Hunter nearly lost everything in an accident that saw her medically discharged from the navy. With the help of the Warrior Fight Club, she's fought hard to overcome her fears and get back in the water where she's always felt most at home. At work, she's tough, serious, and doesn't tolerate distractions. Which is why finding her gorgeous one-night stand on her new dive team is such a problem.

Former navy deep-sea diver Jesse Anderson just can't seem to stop making mistakes—the latest being the hot-as-hell night he'd spent with his new partner. This job is his second chance, and Jesse knows he shouldn't mix business with pleasure. But spending every day with Tara's smart mouth and sexy curves makes her so damn hard to resist.

Joining a wounded warrior MMA training program seems like the perfect way to blow off steam—until Jesse finds that Tara belongs too. Now they're getting in deep and taking each other down day and night, and even though it breaks all the rules, their inescapable attraction might just be the only thing truly worth fighting for.

* * * *

Nothing Without You: A Forever Yours/Big Sky Novella
By Monica Murphy

From *New York Times* and *USA Today* bestselling author Monica Murphy...

Designing wedding cakes is Maisey Henderson's passion. She puts her heart and soul into every cake she makes, especially since she's such a believer in true love. But then Tucker McCloud rolls back into town, reminding her that love is a complete joke. The pro football player is the hottest thing to come out of Cunningham Falls—and the boy who broke Maisey's heart back in high school.

He claims he wants another chance. She says absolutely not. But Maisey's refusal is the ultimate challenge to Tucker. Life is a game, and Tucker's playing to win Maisey's heart—forever.

* * * *

All Stars Fall: A Seaside Pictures/Big Sky Novella
By Rachel Van Dyken

From *New York Times* and *USA Today* bestselling author Rachel Van Dyken...

She *left*.
Two words I can't really get out of my head.
She left *us*.
Three more words that make it that much worse.
Three being another word I can't seem to wrap my mind around.
Three kids under the age of six, and she left because she missed it. Because her dream had never been to have a family, no her dream had been to marry a rockstar and live the high life.
Moving my recording studio to Seaside Oregon seems like the best idea in the world right now especially since Seaside Oregon has turned into the place for celebrities to stay and raise families in between touring and producing. It would be lucrative to make the move, but I'm doing it for my kids because they need normal, they deserve normal. And me? Well, I just need a break and help, that too. I need a sitter and fast. Someone who won't flip me off when I ask them to sign an Iron Clad NDA, someone who won't sell our pictures to the press, and most of all? Someone who looks absolutely nothing like my ex-wife.

He's tall.
That was my first instinct when I saw the notorious Trevor Wood, drummer for the rock band Adrenaline, in the local coffee shop. He ordered a tall black coffee which made me smirk, and five minutes later

I somehow agreed to interview for a nanny position. I couldn't help it; the smaller one had gum stuck in her hair while the eldest was standing on his feet and asking where babies came from. He looked so pathetic, so damn sexy and pathetic that rather than be star-struck, I took pity. I knew though; I knew the minute I signed that NDA, the minute our fingers brushed and my body became insanely aware of how close he was—I was in dangerous territory, I just didn't know how dangerous until it was too late. Until I fell for the star and realized that no matter how high they are in the sky—they're still human and fall just as hard.

* * * *

Hold On: A Play On/Big Sky Novella
By Samantha Young

From *New York Times* and *USA Today* bestselling author Samantha Young…

Autumn O'Dea has always tried to see the best in people while her big brother, Killian, has always tried to protect her from the worst. While their lonely upbringing made Killian a cynic, it isn't in Autumn's nature to be anything but warm and open. However, after a series of relationship disasters and the unsettling realization that she's drifting aimlessly through life, Autumn wonders if she's left herself too vulnerable to the world. Deciding some distance from the security blanket of her brother and an unmotivated life in Glasgow is exactly what she needs to find herself, Autumn takes up her friend's offer to stay at a ski resort in the snowy hills of Montana. Some guy-free alone time on Whitetail Mountain sounds just the thing to get to know herself better.

However, she wasn't counting on colliding into sexy Grayson King on the slopes. Autumn has never met anyone like Gray. Confident, smart, with a wicked sense of humor, he makes the men she dated seem like boys. Her attraction to him immediately puts her on the defense because being open-hearted in the past has only gotten it broken. Yet it becomes increasingly difficult to resist a man who is not only determined to seduce her, but adamant about helping her find her purpose in life and embrace the person she is. Autumn knows she shouldn't fall for Gray. It can only end badly. After all their lives are divided by an ocean and their inevitable separation is just another heart break away...

Discover 1001 Dark Nights Collection Six

DRAGON CLAIMED by Donna Grant
A Dark Kings Novella

ASHES TO INK by Carrie Ann Ryan
A Montgomery Ink: Colorado Springs Novella

ENSNARED by Elisabeth Naughton
An Eternal Guardians Novella

EVERMORE by Corinne Michaels
A Salvation Series Novella

VENGEANCE by Rebecca Zanetti
A Dark Protectors/Rebels Novella

ELI'S TRIUMPH by Joanna Wylde
A Reapers MC Novella

CIPHER by Larissa Ione
A Demonica Underworld Novella

RESCUING MACIE by Susan Stoker
A Delta Force Heroes Novella

ENCHANTED by Lexi Blake
A Masters and Mercenaries Novella

TAKE THE BRIDE by Carly Phillips
A Knight Brothers Novella

INDULGE ME by J. Kenner
A Stark Ever After Novella

THE KING by Jennifer L. Armentrout
A Wicked Novella

QUIET MAN by Kristen Ashley
A Dream Man Novella

ABANDON by Rachel Van Dyken
A Seaside Pictures Novella

THE OPEN DOOR by Laurelin Paige
A Found Duet Novella

CLOSER by Kylie Scott
A Stage Dive Novella

SOMETHING JUST LIKE THIS by Jennifer Probst
A Stay Novella

BLOOD NIGHT by Heather Graham
A Krewe of Hunters Novella

TWIST OF FATE by Jill Shalvis
A Heartbreaker Bay Novella

MORE THAN PLEASURE YOU by Shayla Black
A More Than Words Novella

WONDER WITH ME by Kristen Proby
A With Me In Seattle Novella

THE DARKEST ASSASSIN by Gena Showalter
A Lords of the Underworld Novella

Also from 1001 Dark Nights:
DAMIEN by J. Kenner
A Stark Novel

Discover the World of 1001 Dark Nights

About Monica Murphy

Monica Murphy is the New York Times, USA Today and #1 international bestselling author of the One Week Girlfriend series, the Billionaire Bachelors and The Rules series. Her books have been translated in almost a dozen languages and has sold over one million copies worldwide. She is both a traditionally published author and an independently published author. She writes new adult, young adult and contemporary romance. She is also USA Today bestselling romance author Karen Erickson.

She is a wife and a mother of three who lives with her family in central California on fourteen acres in the middle of nowhere, along with their one dog and too many cats. A self-confessed workaholic, when she's not writing, she's reading or hanging out with her husband and kids. She's a firm believer in happy endings, though she will admit to putting her characters through many angst-filled moments before they finally get that hard won HEA.

For more information about Monica, visit https://www.monicamurphyauthor.com.

On behalf of 1001 Dark Nights,

Liz Berry and M.J. Rose would like to thank ~

Steve Berry
Doug Scofield
Kim Guidroz
Jillian Stein
InkSlinger PR
Dan Slater
Asha Hossain
Chris Graham
Fedora Chen
Kasi Alexander
Jessica Johns
Dylan Stockton
Richard Blake
and Simon Lipskar